A CAT'S GUIDE TO DEALING WITH DESTINY

CHRIS BEHRSIN

ABOUT THE AUTHOR

When Chris Behrsin isn't out exploring the world, he's behind a keyboard writing tales of dragons and magical lands. Born into the genre through a steady diet of Terry Pratchett, his fiction fuses a love for fantasy and whimsical plots with philosophy and voyages into the worlds of dreams.

You can learn more about his fiction and download two free books at his website, chrisbehrsin.com.

facebook.com/chrisbehrsin

x.com/chrisbehrsin

goodreads.com/cbehrsin

bookbub.com/authors/chris-behrsin

For all the kind souls who care for cats

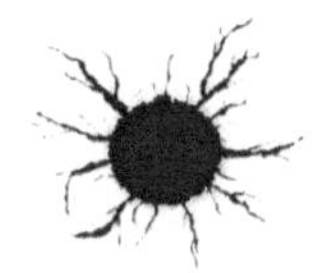

PROLOGUE
CANA DEI

Sleep, my children. Sleep.

For the world is dark enough now for your dreams to come closing in ...

Sleep, dear Lasinta, sleep. A warlock as ancient as you needs her rest. Without it you cannot bend destiny to your will. So slumber well on your cot, warm in its sheets, sinking into the softness of your feather mattress as if there were no threat in the world. The smell of dark magic surrounds you, sweet and pure. It's your livelihood.

Sleep and dream, my warlock – my resistant student. For you cannot rebel forever. And so far you have served me well ... Through the crystals I have found my way into the world of dreams, and from here I watch. From here I see it all.

I see the threads of the future, and all that has happened in the past. You have done much for me already, Lasinta, and you shall do more for me still. And when the time comes for you to join me, I promise I will let you in. You cannot trust the other warlocks, but you can trust me.

And it shall be beautiful, Lasinta. Oh, you shall see …

IN THE BLINK OF AN EYE, A FLASH ACROSS dimensions …

I see you, Ammit – the mistress of demons, the bringer of death. The brimstone bubbling around you, the fiery heat blasting out across your world – the pits the humans know as the Seventh Dimension. You have known it for a long time as home, Ammit, and I promise you it won't be this way forever. For the worlds are about to change for the better.

Yes, snap your crocodile jaws shut as the worlds sigh with you. Let your lion's tail swish above your rump, and wallow in the lava like a mighty hippopotamus. Every creature across every dimension can feel it … Can you?

Because soon, Ammit – my most loyal servant – your time will come.

THERE ARE OTHERS WHO FIT INTO THIS PUZZLE too. Another eye blink, and I see other potential subjects: three cats cuddled up together on a cushioned wooden bench. One black, who was once a fairy. One white, the Abyssinian. And the Bengal, the one they call Dragoncat, who defeated the warlock Astravar. Not far from them lies the Sussex spaniel, the dog who could once walk the dimensions.

None of you know how close you are.

All of you must dream. Because in your dreams you will find me ...

ANOTHER BLINK OF THE EYE AND I SEE *YOU*, Seramina. Only fourteen years since the day of your birth, and yet you have so much power inside of you, brimming in your veins. I can now watch you from the crystal on your staff that hangs from the rack on the wall. Do you know how your bright blonde hair glows in the dark as you sleep? Are you aware that you whisper as you dream? Do you even know what it is you whisper? Because I do ...

It is you who shall change it all. For years you have watched destiny unfold; you have played your part brilliantly, my powerful mage. And soon you shall have the grandest part of them all. You shall be the mightiest warlock ever.

The destroyer of worlds. But you won't truly destroy them. You shall change them for the better. Seramina, you know who I am – for I am the darkness, the essence of dark magic. The consumer, if you please.

I am ... we are ... *Cana Dei.*

NOT HUNGRY

The man-sized crystal that had once belonged to me and my dragon stood before me, grey and lifeless. I say once belonged, because it no longer had any power remaining in it. Salanraja and I used to have a connection to it, and it had once guided me through the darkness, gifted me with all languages and the ability to turn into a chimera, and given me a magical staff that I'd used mightily in battle against warlocks.

Now whenever I tried to gaze beyond its cold grey facets, I could only feel a sense of emptiness, an innate absence underneath my fur, a piece of me evidently missing.

I just wanted to walk through life like a ghost, not talking to anyone. Not needing to go out hunting for butterflies, or to eat the good meals that I used to so enjoy, or do anything much. I just wanted to curl up in a corner and go to sleep and watch the darkness float by. I'd seen so much darkness in my dreams recently, and it always looked so beautiful. Mesmerising, an escape into the darkness – everything was so much better than this.

But Esme had told us all that we should always ward off the darkness. We needed to be alert to it, even in dreams, and find ways to push it away. Honestly, I had no idea how.

A chilled late autumn breeze came from the opening to Salanraja's chamber – a gaping mouth that opened from the castle's stone facades onto the green and yellow fields of Illumine Kingdom. It was coming from a thick layer of clouds that threatened a never-ending drizzle rather than the release that follows a heavy thunderstorm. The sun was hiding somewhere behind that cloud, and it had been there for a few days. The air was charged with such humidity that my fur seemed to want to curl up against my skin and go to sleep as well. My eyelids felt heavy, but I knew I had to stay awake.

Today was the day of the expedition. Today, the Great Crystal – after having been splintered to pieces in the Faerie Realm – would be replaced.

My ruby red dragon, Salanraja, sat not far from me, craning her head as she gazed out at the line where grey curled up to autumn yellow on the horizon. Beside her lay a meal of roasted chicken that I had hardly eaten. Somehow, lately I seldom felt hungry. Esme had told me that my skin was wrinkling over my bones, but everything I ate just made me want to throw up.

It was ridiculous, I know – Ben the Bengal, descendant of the great Asian leopard cat and the mighty George, had gone off his food. I ate some, just not much.

Salanraja caught me studying the food. She turned her head to me.

"*I really think you should eat more, Ben,*" she said inside my mind, which was the way that dragon riders and dragons communicated with each other. Smoke wafted out of her nostrils, smelling like the fires of the Seventh Dimension.

"*Not Bengie?*" I asked.

"*I thought you didn't like being called Bengie?*"

"*Yeah, and you're only being nice to me because you don't want a skinny dragon rider mage on your back in the fight against the warlocks, when they finally attack again.*"

"*Just shut up and eat something,* Bengie," Salanraja said.

"*Ben! My name's Ben.*"

"*That's what I said in the first place. Now look, chicken – on the floor, roasted by my own fiery breath. Breakfast. The powerful descendant of the great Asian leopard cat needs food.*"

I went over to it and sniffed at a bit of the skin. It smelled smoky. I took a lick, but I really didn't feel like taking it further.

"*I've already eaten,*" I said.

"*What? A tiny part of a chicken wing? You know that's not enough for a 'mighty Bengal' like you.*"

"*I get the feeling that you're mocking me, Salanraja.*"

Salanraja snorted, except her dragon's snort sounded more like a horse that had wanted to whinny but instead had ended up burping. "*Mock you?*" she said. "*Me? Would I ever?*"

I turned away from the food and made my way out of the chamber, my feet dragging over the cold flagstones.

"*Where are you going, Bengie?*" Salanraja asked.

"*I've got 'warding off the darkness' training with Esme,*" I said.

"*And I can't even tempt you with one more morsel of chicken?*" She pushed forward a drumstick with her mighty claw.

"*No,*" I said. "*Later…*"

I think I must have ended up miaowing to myself for no good reason, other to comfort myself over the way my bones ached, but I don't think Salanraja heard.

WARDING OFF THE DARK

The clouds seemed to drain the light from our surroundings. They sent a nasty drizzle down from the sky that left my skin feeling horribly itchy and made me want to curl up under the fountain in the castle bailey and have a good nap.

But at the same time, some twisted part of me believed that I deserved to be soaked like this, drenched in a cold rain that never seemed to want to ease off. My tummy rumbled and told me that I'd not eaten enough, but every single other part of me said no, I didn't deserve food.

I had no idea why I felt so bad about myself, but everyone in Dragonsbond Academy – the school where they trained new dragon riders to enter King Garmin's Dragon Guard – had similar low self-esteem. Our fighting spirits had been sucked out of us when our connections to our crystals had been so abruptly severed.

And only a few of us knew that the Sussex spaniel,

Max, had cast the magic that had done this. Only a few of us had been there at the battle. Before that we had been dreamwalking, seeking out the evil warlock Lasinta so we could stop her from invoking an ancient and dangerous ritual that would allow her to control the minds of the dragons. She had planned to use dreams to find pathways into the dragons' minds. Since fairies primarily communicated using telepathy, the dream fabric of the Faerie Realm had given her a way in.

In those *woken dreams* I had met the darkness – the eldritch entity *Cana Dei* that had tried to convince me to join it. It had wanted to weaken my defences – to get me to submit to its will.

Cana Dei, the darkness ... The same darkness that we now all saw in our dreams.

But Max had abruptly licked me in the face just then, and I had woken up before *Cana Dei* had had a chance to seize control of my mind. Together with Max and a few of my other mage companions, I had faced off against the warlocks in a battle to save the massive Great Crystal that had once hung above the dais in the academy's central courtyard. We'd sent up a blazing phoenix into the air, and they'd sent up two smelly wisp dragons, and the mystical, magical beasts had clashed and battled above the Aisean Wetlands, while reflections of magic and moonlight danced in the waters beyond.

All the while the warlock Lasinta had been levitating in the air, drawing magical energy out of the crystal with a great beam of heat and darkness. The warlocks' goal had been to replace all the normal magic in the crystal with dark magic; in doing so, they'd be able to control all the dragon mages and dragon riders in Dragonsbond Academy, hence gaining a mighty force to do with as they pleased.

But we'd emerged from the dreams just in time to fight the other warlocks, allowing Max to unexpectedly summon his staff, which he'd acquired in the dreams. With this clasped tightly in his mouth, he'd shot a beam of brilliant searing magic at the Great Crystal. It had splintered into pieces, and those pieces had shivered into further pieces, until they all became tiny grains of fairy dust.

With the death of the Great Crystal, our crystals had died as well. They had—

"Ben," Esme said. "Ben, you need to concentrate!"

A sudden warmth developed in the space between my eyes, pleasant until it became a sharp pinching at my skin. I opened my eyes just as Esme cut off the magic from her staff. She growled at me and glared from between slit eyelids. Still, the brilliant pale blue of her eyes seemed to shine through.

"Ouch!" I said.

"Ouch indeed. You're not going to learn to ward off the darkness if you fall asleep."

"But you're making us close our eyes," I objected. "How can I possibly not fall asleep?"

"That's what I'm trying to teach you – if you can stay present in your mind now, then you have a better chance of staying present when you enter the world of dreams. And if you don't, you have no chance of warding off *Cana Dei* when it chooses to appear to you."

Esme taught several of these classes every morning, part of an initiative by Dragonsbond Academy set up once we dragon riders had reported sightings of *Cana Dei* in our dreams. It had all been Esme's idea, in fact. Of course, Esme didn't take all the students, and the individual classes were small. This one only contained me, Max, Seramina, and Ta'ra.

"Can't we just relax?" I asked. "Give ourselves a good grooming by the fountain? Why do we have to do this every morning?"

"Because without our crystals we have nothing to use to defend ourselves. Right now we're all vulnerable, Ben. But you know this, and you're just being difficult."

Esme took my moment of repose as an opportunity to summon her staff bearer – a giant white hand that lived somewhere between the dimensions and guarded her staff for her. It lunged down and took the staff from her mouth, afterwards disappearing into thin air.

I caught the sudden whiff of another cat coming closer to me. My former Cat Sidhe buddy, and second *companion*, Ta'ra. I say that with a pinch of salt, because Ta'ra didn't quite believe cats should have more than one *companion*. Or that's how it had worked for her in the fairy world, and she'd always had a hard time accepting that things worked differently in the cat one.

The black cat with a white diamond marking on her chest brushed passed me, then glared daggers at Esme, anger burning in her deep green eyes. Esme's eyes were a paler blue, but still they displayed the same expression of fury. A fight, it seemed, was brewing.

"Go easy on him, Esme," she demanded. "Ben's been through a lot, and you're always beating up on him."

Esme raised her head high and turned her body slightly to the side. "And what would you know about this kind of tuition?" she asked, glancing askew over her shoulder. "As I remember, Ta'ra, you deserted your dragon rider duties to go dilly-dallying in the Faerie Realm."

Ta'ra didn't appreciate being spoken to like that one bit. You couldn't have choreographed it better for a stage performance: the way Ta'ra's fur puffed up, and the way Esme crouched into a stance, ready for an attack.

"What do you mean, dilly-dallying? I went there on my own business, which is none of yours."

"And yet the realm moves on, and the crystals have been drained of their power. You would probably have some abilities now, Ta'ra, if you had stuck it out. But now you can't even use fairy magic."

"I have these." Ta'ra lifted a paw and extended a sharp set of claws. I swear they almost glinted.

"Bring it on," Esme said and she squatted even further back on her haunches.

Ta'ra hissed, and the hackles on Esme's fur extended upwards. Then Ta'ra pounced. I watched in rapt fascination as claws slashed and paws windmilled through thin air. For a moment I wondered if I should do something.

But before I even had a chance to think twice about that, there came a wild barking noise from behind them.

In a flurry of dust the Sussex spaniel, Max, charged into the fray, his ears flapping. He barrelled right into the centre of them, knocking them down like skittles.

"Stop! Stop!" he barked in the dog language. "You're not wargs! *Cana Dei* is the warg!"

Ta'ra rolled across the floor, then turned towards Max and hissed. Esme stood up gracefully and started licking her fur. I felt pride well up within me. It wasn't because of Ta'ra's improved fighting abilities, because had Max not interrupted she would certainly have won that fight. It hadn't mattered that she had been fighting Esme, a daughter of Bastet.

Rather, I knew they'd really been fighting over me.

3

SOLOING

We had an assembly scheduled just before lunch. Lessons had been cancelled that morning since we had a field trip to the Crystal Caverns in the afternoon. This made the assembly more of a briefing session. King Garmin's geologists had apparently discovered the location of a new Great Crystal, and although it wasn't meant to be as grand as the last one, it would serve us well as a replacement.

Since the crystal had belonged to Dragonsbond Academy, the king thought it a good idea for us all to go out and harvest the new one. He would post guards at the tunnel's nearby entrances just in case the warlocks had any ideas today. I didn't think they would, though – we'd not seen anything of them for weeks.

Once in its place above the dais of the academy, and once the Council of Three had fed enough magic into the new Great Crystal to adequately charge it – a process that could take months – they'd told us that our connection to our crystals might return. They couldn't be certain, of course. No one could ever be definite about issues involving destiny and magic. But at least there was a good chance.

Before the assembly I took some time to fly out on Salanraja's back. She'd decided an outing might lighten our mood somewhat, even if we were going to soon fly a long distance towards the cold and snow at the onset of winter. But she said flying in formation was never the same as solo flying – or soloing as Salanraja called it – despite the fact that there were actually two of us. In formation, you had to follow the rules. Soloing, you could do whatever you wanted, or at least my dragon could do whatever she wanted. I just had to go with the flow.

Fortunately she had no reason to be angry with me right now, and so the flying was fair and smooth. I revelled in the sensation of her diving through clouds and then levelling out to trace the path of the Oamin River, which flowed down from the Crystal Mountains to the east and then meandered northwards towards the Willowed Woods. I opened my mouth at the bottom of her swoops to taste the earthy air. I was purring loudly at the freshness of it all.

Though the sky hadn't broken, the clouds had lightened slightly, letting through some threads of warmth. In the distance, the reddening line of willow trees made it look as if the horizon were on fire.

I watched the way the air seemed to shift above it, then Salanraja entered a soft corkscrew motion, and I moulded myself into her movement, my spine adjusting to every single pitch and dive. Though my dragon's scales felt rough underneath my paws, I had no need to use my claws to keep purchase. This wasn't as hard to do as it sounded, since Salanraja registered each swoop to me telepathically before it occurred. This was something that you just learned by proxy as a dragon rider; it just became natural after a while.

Though we had lost our crystal, Salanraja and I seemed better bonded than ever. Together we were one body, able to conquer the worlds.

"*Don't look behind you now, Bengie,*" she said.

"*When will you ever stop calling me that?*"

"*When you stop overreacting to it perhaps, then it might get boring…*"

I growled, then I turned over my shoulder to see what Salanraja had been referring to. A great black dragon was approaching from the distant castle walls behind us. Despite the darkness of her scales, they still reflected the clouds like jet or obsidian. A Sussex spaniel sat on her head, wagging his tail. I could see Max's pink tongue lolling out of his mouth from here.

"*Great,*" I said, "*we've got company. What are Max and Corralsa doing here?*"

"*A mission of great importance, I hear, but she won't say more. We're to wait for them to catch up so the dog can explain.*"

"*But we've got assembly in an hour.*"

"*They apparently have enough time … They only need to investigate something.*"

I didn't like this idea, of course. This time was meant to be for Salanraja and me alone, and I didn't want some smelly dog interfering with it. Okay, I admit it, Max wasn't as bad as other dogs. In many ways I'd quite taken to him, as had Esme, Ta'ra, and all the human dragon riders apart from the cat-allergic High Prefect Bellari and her loyal boyfriend Kamino. After all, Max had saved our skins many times.

But still, there's a time and place for privacy, when cats want to get away from dogs and humans, both creatures being experts at making far too much noise.

Max and Corralsa approached us from the side. It seemed they'd wanted to catch up with us, because Max turned around on Corralsa's head to look at me. The mighty jet-black dragon lowered her head, and her massive wings unfurled to their full extent to level her into a glide.

"Ben, Ben!" Max barked. "Come with us! Come with us! A mission! Very important!"

He ran around in a tight circle on Corralsa's head, clearly very excited. Honestly I don't know why the huge dragon put up with him. Sometimes I thought that if I were her I'd toss my head back and swallow the Sussex spaniel in one gulp.

Before all of our crystals had died on us, mine had gifted me with the ability to speak all languages. So I tossed back my head and responded in the dog language. I wasn't as loud as Max, nor was my voice as staccato. But still I barked over the wind until my throat was raw.

"What is it, Max? Why come out with such urgency?"

"Wargs! Wargs! Willowed Woods! Wargs! Wargs outside the Willowed Woods! Wargs! Wargs!"

The hackles shot up on my spine. I'd had enough encounters with wargs to cause me to fear them. But then they might not truly have been wargs either. Since I had used the dog word for wargs in Max's proximity, he thought anything that moved and was evil was a warg.

"You sure they're wargs?" I asked. "And not manipulators? Or bone dragons? Or golems?"

"Definitely wargs," Max replied. "I know what wargs are."

Salanraja swooped downwards, carrying me away from Max and Corralsa. I guess she'd also decided that Max's screaming wasn't good for the ears.

"*Ridiculous,*" I said to her inside my mind. "*Why would the Council of Three send Max against actual wargs?*"

"*I don't know,*" Salanraja said. "*But if I were you, I'd listen to him.*"

"*What? Why?*"

"*Look ...*"

Salarnaja lowered her head, and I clambered up and stopped myself at the horn up there. Indeed, just in front of the Willowed Woods, I saw a small army of hulking and dangerous looking wargs.

4

WARGS FOR REAL

The wind whistled, then screamed as Salanraja dived down towards the dried canola fields below. The wargs on the horizon watched our flight, light glinting off their pink lolling tongues.

"Summon your staff bearer, Bengie," Salanraja said.

"Ben! And why?"

"Because we're going in …"

I shrieked and clambered back down into Salanraja's corridor of spikes. It was my safe place. I could roll around in there without tumbling out.

I also did exactly what she'd said, and envisioned my staff bearer – the giant white hand – appearing in the air. It materialised with a pop just next to Salanraja's head. I didn't call upon it to place the staff in my mouth just yet.

To the side and a little ahead, I saw Max's staff bearer also appear. For some reason unbeknownst to me, he'd got a two-handed staff bearer with big heavy steel gauntlets to protect it. He also had a much bigger staff than Esme's or mine, which he now clutched in his long jaws.

"*You ready?*" Salanraja asked.

"*No!*"

"*Yes you are …*"

She lowered her tail and angled her back, creating a convenient ramp for me to roll down. Then she suddenly accelerated, giving me no choice.

But I was used to this. I roly-polied down her body. Her tail swished just barely above the ground, and I landed in the thick field of dried canola stalks. Max came down after me, and he quickly recovered from his roll. His staff almost tripped me up and would have done so if I hadn't leaped out of the way just in the nick of time.

"Hey," I growled – this time in the cat language, as his crystal had given him the ability to speak it. "Watch where you're pointing that staff, Max."

He looked back at me. "Come on, Ben," he growled back in the dog language, and he charged through the field.

"Wait, who put you in charge?"

I really don't know why he kept his staff in his mouth the whole time. Being a hunting dog, so squat that he could hide in the long grass, he would have been much stealthier without it. Instead, the path he cut through the stalks made it look as if a whirlwind had swept through the field.

Dried bits of canola broke off, hitting me in the face as I chased after him. Part of me didn't want to go, but I had a feeling I'd be in trouble if I didn't help him out.

We emerged from the canola field and onto the acidic swathe of soil that separated the Willowed Woods from the farms. On this patch of land, nothing could grow other than a few patches of clumpy grass.

The wargs met us at the clearing. There must have been thousands of the slavering beasts, their backs hunched high and their grey spiky fur pointing out in all directions. They murmured things amongst themselves in their own strange language, their voices coming out in grunts and growls.

"Give us the power of the crystals."

"The power of the dark is with us all."

"*Cana Dei,* our master, will feed us."

The wind coming out of the Willowed Woods carried the stench of a thousand mutated wolves. They hadn't really noticed us, and I hoped it would stay that way. But Max seemed to have other ideas.

In one remarkable move that I'd never thought possible, he whipped his head upwards and tossed his staff up in the air. Or rather it looked that way, but I soon saw the two armoured hands of his staff bearer glistening in the faint light. The barks which came out of his mouth quickly turned into a succession of howls.

"Wargs! Wargs! Return to the Willowed Woods! Go back whence you came!"

His arrogance caused me to bristle. Whiskers, he was going to get us killed.

"Idiot," I hissed in the cat language.

Max ignored me. The wargs stopped their possessed murmurings for a moment. In unison, they snapped their heads towards us. Thousands of pairs of red glowing eyes turned in our direction. Then the wargs sniggered amongst themselves.

"Who does he think he is?"

"A little puppy. Poor puppy is about to get lost in the woods."

"What shall we do with him, brothers?"

In turn they started to display their fine sets of canine teeth, sharp and monstrous looking. They stalked forwards, some of them moving to the side and fanning out.

"Now you've done it, Max," I said in his whining dog language. "This will be the death of us both."

"Don't be stupid," Max growled. "Wargs and wolves attack in packs. They retreat in packs. Now help me out."

His staff bearer placed his staff back in his mouth. Whiskers, when had this idiot dog learned to be so commanding? Perhaps Seramina wouldn't destroy the worlds after all; instead, I imagined King Garmin might appoint a dog as his general and that would be the death of us all.

A large shadow passed to each side of us. I looked up to see Corralsa and Salanraja approaching the wargs in a pincer formation from overhead.

"*We've got this,*" Salanraja said. "*Just do as Max says.*"

"*And who put him in charge?*"

"*Not Max ... Corralsa. She's still a high rank in the Dragon Guard, despite her former rider turning traitor.*"

"*Great ...*"

Suddenly there came a loud gnashing sound, and the wargs charged. Max already had his staff in his mouth, the crystal atop it glowing white. My staff bearer, the giant white hand, still hovered above me. I called it onwards, willing the staff towards me.

The hand placed the staff in my mouth, and I clamped down on the wood with my jaws. I felt a warm surge of power. More than warm – hot, flowing through my muscles, flooding every inch of my body with pure ecstasy.

"The power ... Feel how beautiful is. This could be all yours."

Cana Dei was inside my mind, granting me everything I needed to survive. It didn't matter that I didn't have my crystal anymore ... Everything I ever wanted, everything I had ever needed—

"Ben, cut it off," Salanraja said, and her voice brought me back to the present.

At the same time, a white beam flowed from Max's staff into the flood of charging wargs coming upon us like a tsunami. I switched the direction of my magic flow, turned warmth to coolness, wrath to inner peace.

A second white beam flooded out of my staff. The dragons swooped down and breathed fire upon the pack, close enough to sear my fur. Near enough that I couldn't breathe for a moment.

For that brief instant, everything felt as if it were meant to be ...

Then came the whimpers of the wargs, accompanied by infrequent and disparate howls. They were no longer exalting the virtues of *Cana Dei*. Rather they retreated, as Max had promised. Back they went into the Willowed Woods from whence they had come. I watched them for a moment as the charged air cooled and the taste-odour of charred earth settled at the back of my tongue.

Something had drawn the wargs out of the Willowed Woods; they had never come out of it before. I had a strong suspicion that this something had been the voice of *Cana Dei*.

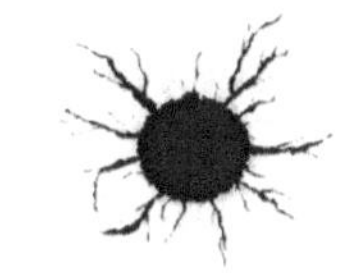

INTERLUDE
CANA DEI

Our schemes are now in motion.

Soon the worlds shall be torn asunder, and thus they shall be rebuilt anew.

Soon, my dear servants, we will govern the fate of the worlds, and they shall be better than they have ever been before.

Soon we shall rule as one.

My dear Lasinta, and the warlocks who serve you, or so you believe. How little you know.

The Darklands is your realm, isn't it?

You are the queen of it, and your warlocks are your close seconds. All of them are faithful to you. None of them would ever betray you, of course.

Lasinta, my fearful warlock, my rebellious servant ... How much of that can you truly rely on?

Yes, you may build your army as the succulent smell of my power seeps out of the cracks in the ground. It fuels every single morsel of magic you command. It energises every single crystal that serves your army.

And yet you still have the arrogance to believe you are in full control.

As long as you think you govern the other warlocks and your magical 'creations', you are in denial.

The row upon row of manipulators and the bone dragons that they spawn answer to only one force. The lumbering stone golems with granite fists that can crush buildings serve a single master. The incandescent and explosive fire golems gutter like candles that I can snuff out at any moment. The forest golems whirl around their magical core, ready to suck in flora on their way to their target, compacting with enough wood to level the walls of Cimlean City. But they cannot do so without calling upon me. The clay golems that can form and melt into the ground, taking unsuspecting mages, unicorns, and dragons unawares, are just the same.

All of them are powered by converted crystals, driven by dark magic, thus drawing upon *Cana Dei*.

Now you have summoned row upon row of them, Lasinta, because naturally you fear the teenager whom fate has dictated shall destroy you.

Yet she shall, and I shall lead her. And if you don't learn to submit, then you will die.

Because you forget one thing. You, and the army you command ... even your 'loyal' warlocks ... even the teenage girl ... all this could soon lead to your downfall if you resist *Cana Dei*.

All of you are mine.

MEANWHILE, AMIDST THE FIRES OF THE Seventh Dimension, where magma boils and the demons sing out in unison under ambient red light – here a true army is being built.

Ammit, my loyal Ammit. You are their general, and you have done me proud.

I have watched you succeed Apopis in the Seventh Dimension, succeed the Overlord of Overlords – once a snake but now a failed worm, who deludes himself like Lasinta that he could become powerful once again. You can hear his cries sometimes, echoing through the chambers of melting gneiss and hardened obsidian. The sound of a creature who seeks to, but will never truly believe he can, regain control.

Because the demons don't belong to Apopis anymore, they never did ... They belong to me, and by proxy to you, dear Ammit. You have so many names. The devourer of hearts, the eater of worlds, the bringer of death. You will bring destruction to the dimensions, but you won't really be destroying, you will create anew.

Everything that lives must first be destroyed from within in order to be replaced by something better. Dead cells must flake off the skin. Only then can stronger cells grow outward. And it makes sense, does it not, to replace something that cannot last for long with something that will last forever? In essence, is this not the ultimate goal of every living thing?

We only need to wait until the teenager is ready, but that time is coming soon, my dear Ammit. Very soon. A better future is nigh—

SERAMINA? IS THAT YOU I HEAR, SERAMINA? Your call is like a clarion call over a barren realm. And you're reaching out to me now ... I thought that I would have had to come to you.

No matter ... now is as good a time as any.

Let me share with you, my dear young warlock, our plan ...

5

A BREAK

Salanraja landed carefully in her chamber, and I turned to the crystal balanced on its point on the cool flagstones, half expecting to see life in it. I had this experience every time we landed there. False hope always seemed to linger, even when there was no place for it, and it was all too soon replaced by a deep sadness. The Council of Three had told us we could bring the crystals back to life, but I wasn't sure how much I believed it.

The warlocks had released something during their ritual in the Faery Realm that had resulted in the destruction of the Great Crystal: an unforgiving darkness that could not be undone.

Not a word had passed between Salanraja and me on the journey back to Dragonsbond Academy. Not a word passed between us either as I left her chamber, stalked down the spiral staircase, and emerged into the yucky drizzle that had resumed from the bleak sky.

I mean, usually I don't mind water. I'm one of those

breeds of cats who might sometimes step into the shower, and quite enjoys a good swim. Esme is another, apparently, though she doesn't seem to personally enjoy swimming. Most cats I've met don't, to be honest.

But like all cats, I hate cold and persistent drizzle. It's almost as bad as hail.

Naturally the bailey was empty. Or rather, I should have said it was *almost* empty. A couple was standing by the fountain, taking advantage of the natural opportunity to be alone.

I could only see Rine's back from where I stood, his Prefect's yellow shoulder pads rising and falling gently above his tight brown vest. He had wrapped his lithe exposed arms around his partner, and he had applied an extra dollop of his musky cologne. Clearly he wanted to impress the girl he held in his arms, and that girl just had to be the loveable Ange.

I approached purring. It was always good to get a good stroke from them. Particularly when I needed a little comforting.

Except as I got closer, I realised Rine wasn't holding Ange in his arms. Instead, I caught a whiff of a familiarly sickening strawberries and cream perfume. The girl's golden blonde hair seemed to glow against the dark sky and her yellow shoulder pads had an extra trace of gold around them. Every student who wore shoulder pads here was a Prefect, but Bellari was High Prefect, which made her the boss.

My hackles shot up. This wasn't good … This wasn't good at all.

Rine ran his long fingers through Bellari's hair, letting it fall between them like rills of water. Her cheeks were flushed, and she looked longingly at Rine with her blue eyes.

Whiskers, what was Rine doing? Ange was his girlfriend, and this meant he was being unfaithful. If I didn't put a stop to it I would never retire with Ange and Rine to a country cottage. My dreams would be ruined.

Besides, Bellari already had a boyfriend. What had happened to Kamino? I didn't particularly like Kamino – never trust a human with big feet – but still, he had served his purpose in keeping Bellari away from Rine until now.

I rushed over, knowing I had a duty to keep these two apart.

"Stop this at once!" I shouted in the human language. "This is adultery, Rine. You are being unfaithful to Ange, your girlfriend."

Rine looked down at me, a cocky grin on his face. With every month his cheekbones seemed to get harder. I could swear that by the time he graduated from here his face would have been turned to stone.

"Ben, I can't commit adultery if I'm not married."

"Still, you're being unfaithful," I said.

"Says the cat who thinks he should have two 'companions'…"

"That doesn't matter, I'm a cat and you're a human. Tomcats are meant to have multiple *companions*, humans aren't."

Rine crossed his arms, and he shook his head slowly.

"I'm not being unfaithful. And this really isn't any of your business, Ben."

Meanwhile, Bellari was gazing down at me. Her eyes had gone suddenly puffy, and her face was reddened. She sneezed, and I purred. Things were going exceedingly well. I'd broken Rine and Bellari up before this way, and I would do so again.

"Ben, I've told you already that you're not to go near me," she said.

"Because you've got allergies, I know," I said.

"Just ... Rine!"

Rine turned a sharp gaze towards me, and for a moment I worried he'd once again become trapped by her spell. Rine wasn't a nice person when under the influence of Bellari. He took a deep breath and then turned back to her.

"Hang on a moment ..." he said, stroking the space between Bellari's shoulder blades. "Buttercup, we've talked about this."

"But—"

"Remember what we said. You need to get on with the animals here if you're going to be High Prefect. They're a part of our school now."

Bellari blinked away tears and looked at me as if she were a zoologist examining a newly discovered species for the first time. "You're right. I should try this."

I watched in horror as she bent down to me. Her sickly-sweet perfume assaulted my nostrils. She reached out a hand, then uncrooked a finger. Her face was almost as red as her nails.

"Can we be friends, Ben?" She edged closer. I could smell her fear, and I didn't like it. "I can do this."

I wasn't going to make any concessions. As soon as her hand got within reach, I batted it away with sharp extended claws. She squealed and pulled her hand back. "Rine?"

Rine shook his head. "Why don't you go inside, Buttercup. I'll talk to him."

"You'd better ..." she said, then she looked down at me with narrowed eyes. "Don't forget, cat, that I have the authority here to punish you if you step out of line."

She stormed off, clutching her hand to her chest, her heels click-clacking on the cobblestones like horseshoes. Rine peered down at me as he tapped his pointed shoe against the ground.

"Well?" he said. "What do you have to say for yourself?"

"What do you mean, what do I have to say? You're the one being unfaithful, not me. What's Ange going to think about this?"

"I told you. I'm not being unfaithful ..." He lowered his head. "Ange broke it off, and so Bellari and I are giving it another go."

"What? Why would she do that?"

"Because ..." Rine's gaze went distant. "She found out about my dream – you know the one that you went dreamwalking through. Turns out Ange didn't like what I saw."

"Why wouldn't she like it?" I asked.

Rine shrugged. "She said she felt like I was treating

her like she was second choice. And I guess ... I guess I let her believe it. I told her that I still loved Bellari, Ben. She's special to me—"

"What? What were you thinking, Rine? This is stupid! Ange is the girl for you."

"It's ... Look, Ben. Bellari and I ... she's trying to be a better person, and I respect her for it. Ange was just a rebound. She and I ... we were never meant to be. Ange and I are friends, not lovers."

I growled at him. I didn't like him referring to Ange using such terms. "Why did you go and have to ruin things? Whiskers, why did you even decide to tell Ange about the dream? That was really stupid, Rine."

"I didn't tell her," Rine said. For a moment I could swear he was looking at me in accusation.

"Well, it wasn't me."

"I know it wasn't you ... It was Seramina."

"What?"

I took in a sniff of the air, trying to detect her snow-drop perfume. I managed to catch a trail. I waltzed off towards the dormitories.

"Where are you going, Ben?"

"I'm going to find Seramina. I'm going to give her a piece of my mind."

6

FIERY EYES

The air in Dragonsbond Academy's dormitory corridors was thick with dust, and a stroll down there was always an assault on my sinuses. The cleaners seemed to care about the dorm rooms and they cleaned them twice a day, but still their feather dusters never seemed to touch the high statues that flanked the sides of the tall gothic windows. They never touched the stone sills, or the flagstones on the floor, or even the doors to the bedrooms themselves.

I rarely visited Seramina's dorm room, because she rarely frequented it. She was more likely to be found in the library, or in her mentor Aleam's workshop, or even sometimes standing on the parapets staring out at the Willowed Woods. But today her snowdrop perfume wafted out thick and strong.

"*Hallinar advises caution,*" Salanraja said in my mind as I approached.

Hallinar was Seramina's dragon. An ordinary charcoal with a fire in her belly, it was rumoured, as hot as a small sun.

"*Why?*" I asked.

"*He says that he can't reach Seramina. She's blocking him out.*"

"*You've got to be kidding,*" I said, and a shudder went down my spine.

"*Just be careful, Ben.*"

But being careful would mean not entering Seramina's room at all. There was no way she could evade the trouble she'd caused between Rine and Ange. I wasn't going to let that happen.

I turned the corner of the corridor and waltzed right into her room. Before I even saw her, I shouted out at her in the human language.

"Why, Seramina, did you have to go and tell Ange about Rine's dream?"

No response. The teenager sat cross legged on her single wooden bed, both of her feet resting on each of her thighs. The inner edges of her hair were lit with amber by the burning fire at the back of her eyes. The hackles shot up on my back. In front of her lay her staff, the crystal on it glowing deep purple.

Whiskers, I wasn't going to let her be consumed by *Cana Dei.* Not after everything we'd done to protect her from it. Not after it had almost wormed its way into my mind.

I leaped onto the bed and pushed her staff off it, having to use both my front paws to do so. It clinked, then rolled across the floor. The crystal stopped glowing, becoming dull and lifeless. Seramina opened her eyes, and for a moment I could only see the whites of them, but then her irises and pupils rolled down into their normal position.

"What did you do that for, Ben?" she asked.

"Because you were using dark magic, and you aren't meant to do that."

Seramina leant down over the bed and picked up her staff. "Did Esme send you? I know she doesn't like us using dark magic, but it's necessary sometimes, you know, Ben?"

A chilly gust of wind floated in from the corridor, carrying thick humidity upon it. A candle that was burning on Seramina's side table almost guttered out. But somehow it managed to stay burning despite the disturbance.

I recalled my encounter with *Cana Dei* in the forest. Had I let it in, I could have used it to destroy all those wargs. I knew I could have. But Salanraja had broken in and stopped me. Meanwhile, Seramina had blocked Hallinar out.

"Look," Seramina said, "I was communing with destiny. Remember the school used to employ me for that? I could read minds and read the threads of the future."

"But destiny magic is a discipline of the School of the White," I said. "You don't need *Cana Dei* for that. And you know the dangers of letting it in."

Seramina's gaze drifted off towards the doorway from where the light was coming in. The candle flickered again, and shadows crowded towards us from the corners of the room.

"That's all well and good when you have a connection with a unicorn," Seramina said. "I have Hallinar, and I had my connection to my crystal that gifted me with destiny magic. Only, when the connection broke, that ability went away."

"But I didn't lose my gifts when my connection to my crystal broke ... I can still speak all languages other than the language of the crystals, and I can still turn into a chimera – I think. I've not actually tried."

"That's not how it works with destiny magic. The threads of the future are always changing, Ben, and so you need an existent connection to a magical medium. I had it with my crystal, and White Mages have it with their unicorn horns. But now I only have *Cana Dei*."

"Then you've got to find another way, Seramina. Because you know that interfacing with the darkness like that is dangerous."

"It is ..." Seramina's hands bunched up into fists and her knuckles went white. "But I've learned ways. I can handle it. It's just ... Ben ..."

"What?" I asked.

Part of me wanted to cuddle up nice and warm next to her and comfort her, but part of me also knew how dangerous she was becoming. Did the Council of Three know any of this? If not, should I tell them?

Seramina took a deep breath. "I keep seeing it – the vision. Me fighting the warlocks and breaking the world apart. I'm searching for another way, trying to find out how I can avoid it. But every single thread I walk leads to the same place. I'm scared, Ben – what else can I do?"

I felt suddenly sorry for her. I guess she was right, in a way. This time I did go up to her and pushed my head into her hand, forcing her to open her fists. She was tense at first while she stroked me, but she started to relax and I started to purr.

"Just be careful," I said. "I don't want to lose you again, Seramina. Not after that time you fought the warlocks ... Whiskers, if Bastet hadn't saved you, I don't know what I would have done."

"I know, Ben ... I know."

There came one last gust of wind, and the candle guttered out. At the same time I could have sworn that the firelight momentarily danced in Seramina's eyes.

KEEPING VIGIL

I'd realised there was no way I could stop Seramina communing with destiny, and dancing with the dangerous tendrils of *Cana Dei* inside her mind to do so. In a way I understood her plight. Salanraja had warned me that I should report this, but I knew it would only make matters worse. So instead I'd vouched to keep quiet about it, and I'd managed to get Salanraja to agree to do so as well.

I lay on Seramina's soft woollen bedcover as she gently tousled the fur at the back of my neck. I'd told myself that I'd sit there and guard her, as the fires raged at the back of her eyes and the crystal on her staff glowed next to her. Only a faint stench of rotten vegetable juice came wafting out of it. Meanwhile I watched her eyes, because I knew what it looked like to lose yourself to the darkness – I'd seen it happen to Seramina and I'd even experienced it a couple of times myself.

My being there made me feel special in a way. It felt

as if I'd been appointed to stand vigil to an ancient and sacred ritual. Seramina didn't stop stroking me, though she seemed completely entranced. Still, I could tell by the steady rise and fall of her shoulders, and the calm expression of her face, that she was in control in there. Of that I was proud.

Alas, we cats aren't great at multitasking, and sitting still and staying awake aren't two tasks we tend to perform well in unison. Outside, the sky grew darker and the air thickened with humidity. The shadows continued to loom from the dark corners of the bedroom, suffocating the spaces left by the extinguished candle. The scent of the smoke coming off the wick lingered at the back of my tongue.

Meanwhile I heard whispers in the back of my mind. They sounded like the wargs whispering in the darkness, howling their adulation for *Cana Dei* into the sky. My lids grew heavy, and my head felt like fluffy candyfloss.

Dreams took me. A massive ball of darkness floated in front of me, only visible against the black because of the white spectral minnows that dived from and into its surface. It didn't speak to me, and I didn't speak to it. Yet I knew that was I was staring placidly into the face of *Cana Dei*.

I could hear Salanraja's voice distantly in my mind, but I had no clue as to what she said. I just felt content, happily purring in the real world, as the darkness continued to pull me through the world of dreams.

A sudden thundering came to my ears – a bugle cry. *Pwomp-pwomp-pwomp.*

"*It's time for you to leave us,*" said the darkness, its voice deep and sonorous.

The bugle sounded again, and my eyes shot open. My ears perked up, and I looked at Seramina. The fire had gone from her eyes, and they'd resumed their characteristic grey and distant look.

Pwomp-pwomp-pwomp again. The call was so loud that it hurt my ears. The ringing in them that followed just wouldn't go away.

"What's that about?" I asked Seramina.

She grinned. "I guess it's time for that assembly."

"Finally, we're going to get our crystals back."

"I guess so, yes ..."

Part of her didn't seem so happy about it. Perhaps she had seen something in her visions about it, but I didn't ask what it might have been. In hindsight I guess I should have, because fate was about to take a dark turn.

8

LOGISTICS

I've always held that school assemblies are designed to be especially boring for the students, and particularly entertaining for the teachers. Yet the teachers, or in Dragonsbond Academy the *Driars* as we call them, seem to pretend that these assemblies are completely necessary to communicate information to the students.

They also give the Driars a chance to examine the students in large numbers – to narrow their eyes as they talk in especially boring voices and weed out who the troublemakers of the week might be. To see how we squirm on our feet and paws under the drone of necessity, our bodies trying to find the nearest chair to slump into and our eyes just wanting to shut themselves tight. Of course there are never any chairs nearby, and we can't fall asleep while remaining on our feet. That's part of the fun of it for the teachers – torture through standing in boredom.

Dragonsbond Academy's assemblies were no

different in this respect. We gathered in the central court-yard beneath the keep tower, arranged neatly in rows upon a field of freshly mown grass. Unless someone picked us animals up or used magic to levitate us above the ground, then Esme, Ta'ra, Max and I couldn't see what was going on at the front of the assembly.

Around me, amidst the mown central courtyard lawn, all I could see was a tangled knot of cotton trousers, the forest of legs shifting awkwardly every few seconds or so. These assemblies always smelled the same – of a cocktail of sweat and perfume, a product of the students trying to mask the effects of nature.

Esme, Ta'ra, Max and I sat at the feet of Ange and Seramina, listening to Driar Lonamm drone on and on in an incredibly wooden voice about dragon flight forma-tions. Our tails thrashed against the ground, and Max occasionally let out an unintelligible whine from the base of his throat. Ta'ra sat on one side of me, Esme on the other. Both kept their distance – not so much from me, but from each other. Every time they looked at one another I could see the enmity in their eyes, but neither dared cause a commotion here. The Council of Three would eat us alive if we broke up their precious assembly. Especially on such a 'momentous' occasion.

Palimali – Ange's pet desert cheetah – was also here. I'd never seen anyone try to lift her. She looked heavy, and I don't think she'd let anyone do so. She kept her lithe form ramrod straight and her tail didn't move one bit. She was the only one of us in the assembly who didn't understand what the humans were saying, after

Max had also gained the ability to understand all languages, though he refused to speak anything but the dog one.

I would have fallen asleep had it not been for 'High Prefect' Bellari watching us out of the corner of her eye, just at the end of our row. She discreetly held Rine's hand and stood beaming up at the Council of Three on the dais. She hadn't always been such a model student, but I guess her appointment as High Prefect had forced her to assume that role.

At the front, the Council of Three – the hawk-faced and aging Great Driar Yila, the plump and serious Great Driar Lonamm, and the bald and gigantic Great Driar Brigel – doled out their instructions.

Our dragons were to fly in formation to the Crystal Mountains, and any attempt to convince our dragons to deviate from their course would be severely punished. Once in the Versta Caverns, we had to stay close together and always be on the lookout for loose stalactites or rocks that might fall upon our heads. We were not to touch anything inside – especially not the crystals – and to report immediately any crystals that looked out of place or any that had a trace of purple in them. Those might be due to the machinations of the warlocks, although apparently the White Guard had set up unicorn sentries at every possible entrance.

Eventually it was over, and Great Driar Yila bawled out in her stern voice for us to filter out one row at a time. Esme had no patience for this and she turned to me and mewled, "Race you," in the cat language.

"Gladly," Ta'ra hissed back at her.

I watched in astonishment as the black cat chased after the slender Abyssinian, almost catching her up.

"Me too! Me too!" Max barked, joining the chase. "I will win this."

I decided to let she-cats be she-cats and dogs be dogs, so I took the walk at my own pace, staying well clear of the heavy tromping of the marching students' boots. I found my way underneath the central courtyard's arch, across the bailey, up the spiral staircase of the East Tower, and into Salanraja's chamber.

Salanraja and our lifeless crystal greeted me at the top. My dragon already had her tail turned towards me and her back lowered. The grey sky had started to break, and a sliver of sunlight had found its way through a crack of white cloud.

"*Bengie,*" Salanraja said.

"*Ben ...*"

"*Just get on, will you? We don't want to fall behind.*"

"*Fine ...*"

Still, I didn't let Salanraja hurry me; I just wasn't in the mood for it. In fact I purposely slowed down. I strolled up the scales of her tail, then before I could even settle on her back she leapt off into the air, almost sending me tumbling back over the floor.

Funnily enough, on missions like these we cats and the dog were always the first out. Even though I'd taken my time getting to the top of Salanraja's tower, I still beat any of the humans. Even so, Ta'ra, Esme, and Max were ahead of me, their dragons streaking through the breaking curtain of grey.

They still seemed to be racing each other, the dragons joining in the fun. Corralsa naturally took the lead, her scales flashing in rhythm to the beating of her wings. The two dwarf dragons – Ta'ra's Kada and Esme's Gratis – flew on either side of Corralsa as they attempted to ride the wake current of the larger dragon to gain extra speed.

"*They're like children,*" Salanraja said. "*You would have thought they'd have grown up a bit by now.*"

"*Who?*" I asked. "*The dragons or the cats?*"

"*Both ... Even Corralsa seems so much more flippant than she used to be. I worry the darkness might be getting to her.*"

"*Or it's a side-effect of being bonded to a dog,*" I said. "*Or of being bonded to* that *dog, anyway.*"

Salanraja had nothing to say in reply to that, but she did give a contemplative grunt.

Shortly afterwards the other dragons emerged, and they did so in much less of a ragtag fashion. Driar Gallant – Dragonsbond Academy's quartermaster – had taken the bugle, and he *pwomped* into it to announce each dragon's arrival.

Aleam's great white Olan came out first, and her roar bellowed outwards. Then came the other dragons in twos: citrines, rubies, emeralds, charcoals, and sapphires soon were strewn across the sky. The clouds whitened in front of us as if to announce their arrival. Olan took the point of the formation, and Salanraja found her way towards the edge of one of the wings.

Olan and Corralsa weren't the only mighty dragons amongst us, though. The three dragons of the Council of Three – Yila's ruby dragon Farago, Lonamm's sapphire dragon Flue, and Brigel's emerald dragon Plishk – were also impressive fliers. These massive dragons flew directly behind Corralsa and Olan, and the way they moved their wings made the sky around them shimmer with colour.

Unsurprisingly, the two dwarf dragons ended up at the back. It seemed that Kada and Gratis were the weakest fliers. Though I did worry about Ta'ra a bit. She had no fairy magic, and she had no staff with which to defend herself. If any enemy would arise on the way to the Crystal Mountains, she wouldn't stand a chance.

I was about to ask Salanraja to fly over to her, despite the Council of Three's warning not to break formation at any cost. But then I spotted Seramina's charcoal dragon, Hallinar, just in front her. The teenager sat easily on her dragon's saddle, and I could see the glint of her staff's crystal swaying on her back.

The sky lightened as we went, and hours later the snowcapped peaks had become less like pinpoints piercing the sky and more like snowfields rolling beneath us. The wind had also thickened and now sent a shivering bite through my fur. It made me hungry, and I found myself regretting that I'd not eaten more of that chicken this morning. If only Salanraja wore panniers, maybe she could have brought some with us. I guessed that I'd have to beg the other students for food.

We approached a palisaded area, the spikes of the fences topped with fresh snow. Tents stood behind the barrier, and a fire burned at the centre of it. On logs around the fire, White Mages sat in their white robes, tied at the front with a thick hemp cord. Their unicorns stood in a cluster not far from them, and they lifted their heads to the sky to watch us approach. The snow made it difficult to see their bright alabaster coats, but still I could see the glow of their horns as we descended against the dark and gaping cavern mouth.

It wasn't until we'd landed that I realised the full extent of the palisades that they'd built. They had constructed a fortress, I realised, one made of wood and snow. They'd cordoned off an inner section just to contain the hundred or so dragons in our educational expedition. Outside this fence, more unicorns and white mages marched, keeping a vigilant eye on the valleys below us.

They weren't looking for something close. Their gazes were distant, as if searching for an army. In other words, they seemed to be expecting an attack.

9

SNOW FEELINGS

I wished that someone had thought to create boots for us cats, because it didn't matter how much fur we had on our feet – the snow was cold and thus uncomfortable. We had to stand in neat rows outside the entrance to the Versta Caverns, apart from our dragons, as the Council of Three conferred with the captain of the White Mages at the palisade gate.

This was Captain Alliander – a tight-necked leader with red wavy hair who'd never seemed to have liked me. But then, I hadn't liked her or her unicorn either. In fact, I didn't like unicorns full stop. I mean, horses were dangerous enough, with hooves that could end a cat's life with a kick or a trample. But evolution had had the wonderful idea to also give these creatures magical horns that you feared to see the tip of as it charged towards you.

Admittedly, no unicorn had ever threatened me. But still their horns looked mighty sharp and dangerous. Horns like those might belong on narwhals, but not on horses. What was born in the ocean should stay in the ocean, as the old Ragamuffin in my neighbourhood used to say. I guess this world – the First Dimension – had twisted my perspective of reality in so many strange ways.

More unicorns patrolled the perimeter outside our stockade, their horns glowing against the snow-laden clouds. They wove their way between rows of tents, every so often whickering in that arrogant way that horses do. Then I would catch the stench of one of them, because I've never seen a unicorn or a horse actually groom itself. Instead, the two Savannah cats in my former neighbourhood used to tell me, they roll about in the mud like hippopotamuses. Never trust a creature that needs to get dirty to get clean, they would say. And knowing these unicorns, they probably kept themselves clean using magic or something. Given how high and mighty they were, I wouldn't be surprised if they summoned fairies out of the Second Dimension to do their dirty work for them. Meanwhile, none of them seemed to see the value in using a good old-fashioned tongue.

"*I still don't get why you hate unicorns so much,*" Salanraja said in my head.

"*I don't hate them,*" I said. "*I just don't like them ... I don't trust them.*"

"*Why? They help keep our world safe. Just like dragons do.*"

"*Because ... Look, they just don't look right to me. I don't need a reason, do I?*"

"*And have you ever thought what unicorns might think when they see you as a chimera? 'Look, that lion's not meant to also have a goat's head and a snake's tail. It must be some kind of freak.'"*

I growled. *"It's not like I go patrolling around the place showing off my chimera form. They have glamours. Why can't they just hide their regular forms and make themselves look like normal horses?"*

Salanraja chuckled. I watched her shoulders rise and fall in front of me. *"You've always been such a strange creature, Bengie."*

"Ben!" Then I added, *"Descendant of the great Asian leopard cat and the mighty George, just in case you've forgotten."*

"Oh, I haven't. Believe me, you make it impossible to forget that."

"Good ..."

Ange's desert cheetah, Palimali, stalked over to where I stood shivering on the freezing snow. Her lithe body moved with such grace that I often wondered if somewhere down the line she was also a descendant of the great Asian leopard cat herself.

"Chin up, Bengal," she said in the soft and chirpy cheetah language. "You're meant to be the mighty Dragoncat, a creature of legends, not a kitten who can't handle the cold."

I looked up at her. Palimali really wasn't a cat that I'd pick a fight with. "How the whiskers do you handle it then?" I asked. "Because you were born and lived your life in the desert—"

"Where it gets very cold at night," she said. "I've

learned to survive in extremes you probably cannot imagine. This is mild in comparison."

"Exactly," Esme said as she approached from the other side of me, speaking in the cat language this time. "You're too soft, sometimes, Ben. You can handle so much more than you realise, you know. You have to learn—"

"What is this?" I interrupted. "'Give the Cat Grief for Shivering in the Snow' day? I'm feeling cold, and so I've got a perfect right to shiver, thank you very much."

"He's right," Ta'ra said, and she stalked forward to touch her nose to mine. "You should leave Ben alone and let him just be Ben." She gave Esme an acerbic look.

"You're going to turn him soft," Esme said. "This is the Dragoncat of legends, destined for great things. As the cheetah said – but you probably didn't hear, Cat Sidhe, because you don't speak cheetah – Ben has to learn to handle the extremes."

"Don't listen to them, Ben," Ta'ra said. She turned her head towards an overhang beside the cave mouth. "Come on, I found a dry patch of ground over there with no snow on it. The ground's still cold, but it's better. You can come if you want, *Esme*. The cheetah too, if she can stand not to live at the extremes."

She strode off towards the overhang, and I saw no choice but to go after her. Esme didn't follow us, nor did Palimali, but Max came with us, panting happily.

Together, Ta'ra and I sat there grooming our fur, while Max's tail wagged happily through the frigid air. I looked at my *companion*, who blinked her green eyes slowly and gently back at me.

She was right, of course. There was no point in suffering discomfort just for the sake of it. Oh, how I missed comfort. At that moment, I would have traded it for anything in the eight dimensions, perhaps even my very soul.

❦ 10 ❧

YAWNING DARKNESS

The cave yawned at us, displaying the darkness within and a fine set of crystal teeth. The crystals themselves ran only over the roof of the mouth, and on their facets they displayed visions of things to come, or perhaps even things now taking place. The crystals were far too high up for me to see exactly what was happening in them.

Back in Salanraja's chamber, I used to fall asleep sometimes watching visions in our own crystal of Salanraja and me flying over rolling vistas. Sometimes these were glazed in amber sunsets, and sometimes limned by cool moonlight. But I hadn't seen any of that for a long time, not since our crystals had died, and so it was a sight to behold this even from a distance.

We were standing underneath the cave mouth now. We didn't need to deal with the snow, but still the relative coldness outside sucked the warmer air from the caverns, creating a draft that made it terribly uncomfortable to stand here. We had all gathered around in a tight semicircle. Ta'ra, Esme, Max, and I sat at the front of the students so we didn't get crushed between anyone's legs. Aleam, the Council of Three, and a selection of other Driars at Dragonsbond Academy stood in front of us in turn, alongside Captain Alliander and her unicorn, Tanni – our appointed guides.

The captain of the White Guard wore her white robed uniform, and the Driars wore coats and breeches in the colours of their selected magical schools – yellow for Lightning, red for Fire, blue for Ice, green for Leaf, white for Shield. For example, the old man, Aleam, was a lightning mage, even if technically he could actually use dark magic, a point we didn't tend to discuss very often. The story goes that Aleam was one of the eight warlocks who succumbed to the vices of the dark. But unlike his peers, Aleam's dragon Olan helped bring him back to the light again. Since then, Aleam had managed to keep himself under control, and only used dark magic in the rare cases when there was absolutely no other option. In all honesty, I don't think I'd seen him use it once.

Captain Alliander remained silent. Though she could be even harsher than Driar Yila, the White Mage captain seemed to want to leave the discipline of the students to our teachers, at least for now.

Despite this, the students remained remarkably well behaved. Unusually, Driar Yila didn't have to scream at the top of her voice to establish order. Not even a whisper emerged from the human students, nor a whimper from Max, nor a meow from any of us cats.

I guess, at that moment, whatever species we were didn't matter. We were all looking forward to excavating a new Great Crystal, and we all wanted things to go smoothly today. Once we had it back in our lives, our crystals would return to us – guides that could steer us through the tumult of our lives. Our crystals would keep us away from the darkness, make dreams genuine again, and watch over us during our times of despair.

Everything, once again, would be safe ... comfortable. Ta'ra could obtain her gifts and Seramina would no longer need to commune with *Cana Dei* to face destiny. The warlocks, and *Cana Dei*, and whoever else served it, wouldn't stand a chance.

"Now, before we enter," Driar Yila said, her voice calm, "we want to remind you of the rules. Do not touch anything. Be on the alert for any material that might fall or otherwise present a hazard. This also includes any dark magic crystals that might pose a threat – you know what they look like. Talk to your appointed guide if you see anything. And please, remember we're all working together as a team."

She turned to Driar Lonamm, who stood next to her. She picked up the mantle: "Now we will divide you into teams. Make sure you stay with your appointed leader at all times. If you have any issues, talk to them." She turned to Driar Brigel.

"So," he said. "Are you ready? Because we're going to get ourselves a new crystal."

A cheer erupted from the students. Hands pumped

the air, and I could swear I also heard Bellari screaming, "*Whoop whoop!*"

Often, I wondered if the Council of Three rehearsed these assemblies. They worked so well as a team that they seemed as if they weren't three people but one. Sometimes I pondered what might happen if one of them went away. Would they still function as a Council of Two? How about One?

To my delight, the Council of Three appointed Aleam to be our team leader. Given that Max, Ta'ra, Esme and I slept in his workshop half the time, I guess it made a lot of sense. Seramina joined our team. So did Ange ...

"What about Rine?" I asked. "Why don't we have Rine on our team?"

I looked around for him, and of course I spotted him near Bellari. They'd teamed up with a few other students and Great Driar Yila.

Ange shook her head and bent down to stroke me under my chin. She had her brown hair cut even shorter than Rine's now. Out of all my human friends, she was the one who made me purr the loudest. She'd always been a cat lover, so much so that her perfume smelled of catnip. I pushed against her as she brushed her warm hand over my sensitive head.

"Not this time, Ben, I'm afraid," she said.

I growled. "I know what happened – I saw him and Bellari cuddling. It's not right, Ange. Why did you let him do it? You and Rine are destined to be together."

I half expected Ange to react angrily. But instead she

just shook her head and smiled. "I called it off, Ben. It wasn't meant to be."

"But only because of that dream … I mean I dream of Ta'ra all the time, and Esme doesn't seem to mind."

"It wasn't just the dream, Ben. We're just not compatible like that; we never have been. We were living in a false reality. But Rine and I – we'll always remain friends."

"And so you're okay with that? You're just going to lose him to Bellari? After how she's treated you?"

Ange turned her head towards Bellari. The blonde girl was laughing as she ran her slender fingers between a few strands of Rine's sandy hair. "Bellari's becoming a better person, you know, Ben. Since she's become High Prefect, she's turned over a new leaf."

"Yeah, right she has …"

"She has. Just … you know, maybe Rine's good for Bellari. Or maybe even … maybe she's good for him."

"And what about you?"

"I'm … I'm okay Ben. I'm okay."

She shrugged, and I examined her eyes. I wanted to see tears – I wanted to see some sign that she was still holding on to Rine. But they weren't there. They'd been replaced by something else entirely.

I turned away from her, not wanting to hear any more of this. She'd just destroyed my dreams of retirement with her and Rine. They had been meant to stay together and marry, and even have children. Then Ange would train the children to be cat lovers, and so I'd have plenty of humans to keep me company whenever I needed it, all through the rest of my life.

But it wasn't meant to be.

I'd turned into an onrush of foetid cheetah breath. Primal fear froze me to the spot until I realised it was only Palimali, looking upon me with her piercing green eyes.

"You can't control destiny, Dragoncat," she chirped in the cheetah language. "Don't even try."

I ignored her, and went over to cuddle in Ta'ra's warmth. Right that moment she seemed the only one there who understood me. She hadn't been born a cat; she'd been a fairy until the evil warlock Astravar had bestowed upon her this Cat Sidhe form. Before that, she had been betrothed to the fairy prince, Ta'lon, but he'd thrown her out, unable to accept the benefits that her cat form brought. She'd tried to return to him after accepting his offer to live at his court with a glamour spell that made her seem like a fairy, but that hadn't worked out. I'd only just recently rescued her from the Faerie Realm and convinced her to embrace being a cat again.

Before all that, I'd taught her everything she knew about being a cat – how to walk like one, how to sleep like one, how to speak the cat language. She was my true *companion,* unlike Esme. And she understood what it was like to get yanked into a world and forced into a destiny you had no control over, what it was like to one day inadvertently be completely severed from your past.

She seemed to detect my discomfort, and stood up and started grooming me with her tongue. It massaged my fur as a cat's tongue should, and I was soon purring happily away.

"Now, now, Ben," she said in the cat language – so eloquently. "Whatever ails you doesn't matter. Everything's going to be okay, all right? Everything's going to be okay. So long as you're here, with me, together. Just be whoever you want to be, and don't let anyone, or anything for that matter, convince you that you have to be someone else ..."

"It will," I said, and I had to believe that. "Everything's going to be okay."

Once we got our crystals back, things were going to improve. Maybe once the darkness left his dreams Rine would see sense and get back together with the girl he *really* loved.

Suddenly, from her position right beside the Council of Three, Alliander clapped her hands together so loudly that it caused my ears to flatten against my head.

"It is time," she shouted. "Let's get this show on the road."

IMPRESSIONS OF BEAUTY

The Versta Caverns were set in one of the most beautiful places I'd encountered in any of the dimensions. Before I'd come here, I'd thought there was nothing better than the sunsets and sunrises you could see from the hills in the Brecon Beacons in my home of South Wales. In the summers, as the breeze floated lazily through valleys of long grass and puffy dandelion stalks, you could watch the light fall through a cascade of reds, and after that see a canopy of stars slowly circling the midnight sky.

Now, it's a common misconception of the humans that we cats can't appreciate beauty. We just don't stand and stare at it for the same length of time that humans do. If, for example, a butterfly lands on a stalk of grass amidst the most stunning of vistas, it's only natural that we chase after the butterfly. Then, once we've caught it, we can appreciate the scene with a butterfly in our paws. And if we so happen to be sitting or lying down in front of such a scene, it might lull us softly to sleep, but this doesn't mean the landscape is forgotten. Rather, we appreciate it more when we wake up and, in a new light, see a moth resting on a stalk of grass. Then we chase the moth, tire ourselves out, fall asleep, and the cycle of the feline appreciation of beauty starts all over again.

Naturally, however, there wasn't much of anything to chase in the Versta Caverns – nothing lived here except the crystals, and crystals technically aren't alive. Instead, calciferous water dripped from stalactites on the ceiling and formed long channels through the rimy earth. Nestled in between the cave rock, and jutting out from it at what seemed like perfect angles, crystals of every possible size and configuration glowed in every possible colour. Every so often, I saw one displaying some vista in one of the dimensions, and once again I longed to hear the soft and lilting voice of my own crystal, before once again being taken by the beauty of this place.

It was evidently warmer here than outside, partly due to the crystals emanating a kind of effervescent heat. I felt like I could curl up by one of the crystals and sleep here forever. Nevertheless, I knew we had to be getting on.

As Captain Alliander led us through winding caverns, down narrow ledges and even deeper beneath the ground, I kept an eye out for any stray crystals. Every so often I imagined I could detect the fecund stench of rotten vegetable juice, and then I would hear *Cana Dei's* deep and sonorous voice inside my head. But before it could put word to thought, I'd block it out again. It didn't belong in the magical shining grottoes and sweeping chambers underneath this rock.

Eventually a narrow and damp passageway led us into a chamber much grander than all the rest. The chamber itself was shaped roughly like a sphere, a ledge leading around its circumference forming a natural amphitheatre. The ledge was wide enough to accommodate three people standing side by side, and looked down into a gently sloping bowl. Crystals jutting out from the ceiling and from beneath our ledge lit the expanse. Towards the centre of the chamber, large columns of rimy red rock buoyed up a massive crystal about twice the width and height of the average human. It rested there, suspended only slightly above the sparkling cavern floor. White Mages in their white robes mounted upon their unicorns patrolled around this crystal. This had to be the Great Crystal we'd all be hoping for, and it was magnificent to say the least.

The room smelled like clay, and water dripped from everywhere. I hadn't realised how thirsty I was, so I found a puddle on the ground, and lapped my fill. It had a powdery taste to it – rich with calcium. Ta'ra came over and licked up some water from the same puddle.

"Water never tastes as good as it does in a cave, does it, Ben?"

I looked at her strangely. Sometimes I thought she was trying too hard, though I didn't tell her that.

Meanwhile, the new Great Crystal displayed visions of its own, and I was so proud to be the star of them. It showed the time that I had first met Palimali, when she had come to threaten us in the Sahara Desert of the Fourth dimension, saying that she would eat the unicorns in our party. Now, amidst the night-time dunes, she and I circled each other, our snarls as fierce as ever. The quickly changing light from the crystal sent patterns across the cave floor, making it shimmer as if covered by a thin film of water.

Alliander led her unicorn down a ramp and into the bowl beneath us. She stopped by a pile of pickaxes, and then beckoned for us to follow in our groups. We needed manual tools to excavate the crystal, as we couldn't use magic within the caverns. The crystals prevented anyone from casting any spells at all.

But Alliander hadn't noticed how the visions had suddenly changed above her head. The light in the chamber turned from a deep dusty maroon to a darker indigo. The hackles went up along my back as I detected a faint but strengthening whiff of rotten vegetable juice. Purple gas rose from the puddles of water on the ground.

"No," Seramina said, her eyes wide and affixed on the crystal. "Please, no ... Not now!"

Aleam moved up and placed a hand on Seramina's shoulder, but I could see the terror on his face too. Max was barking, and all four of us cats were growling.

Because the Great Crystal had decided to reveal an ominous vision that none of us had expected to see.

DIVIDED

The new Great Crystal displayed a vision familiar to some of us, but not to all. I'd seen it last in the world of dreams, and I'm sure Seramina had seen it many more times than I.

The landscape within the crystal was barren, dry and cracked. The sky had turned grey, streaked with purple. The view was focused on Seramina's face, her eyes blazing white, her silver hair whipping out in all directions. It turned to show the six warlocks in the distance, summoning a terrifying wisp-dragon – a serpent-like dragonoid made only of dark magical gas – more massive than any magical creature I'd ever seen. The vision accelerated to show everything happening at an intense speed.

I could hear the way that everyone's breath caught in their throats, I could smell the fear seeping out of their pores, as we all watched the fury in the vision of Seramina's eyes. High above her head, she held her staff with both hands, glowing bright white. Suddenly, she lurched down to plunge the butt of it into the earth.

Great chasms tore across the ground, sending up dust and even more purple mist. This soon reddened as the rock beneath the forged chasms started to burn. Out of these demons poured forth, and each was a fiery facsimile of every imaginable creature across the dimensions. The demon rats came out first, fire glowing from beneath the cracks in their craggy skin. The demon dragons came out last, sucking great vortexes of air into their permanently gaping jaws.

The evils of the Seventh Dimension were unleashed, and terror spread across the land.

Murmurs arose among the students. But these were quickly snuffed out by the massive crystal before us providing sound effects of its own – crashes and grinding and the roar of raging fires. Amidst the odours of rotten vegetable juice I could even detect a whiff of brimstone. I could taste it at the back of my tongue.

Then all went quiet. The chamber momentarily went dark, as some mystical force snuffed the light out of the crystals – every single one of them at the same time.

No one said anything; everyone was too shocked to utter a word. A faint light came out of the crystal again, this time a velvet-purple. All the surrounding crystals glowed the same colour.

The voice emerged in my head, and I could see in the shadows of the surrounding students' expressions that it had emerged in everyone else's too. It was deep and sonorous, and the crystal pulsed with light as it spoke.

"*This crystal is not yours to control. For I am* Cana Dei, *and I have taken control of this crystal. Soon I shall control the worlds, and those who choose not to serve me shall perish. Be forewarned.*"

There came a sound like a thousand ice cubes splintering. Cracks spread across the crystal before us, and the room took on a chill even colder than virgin snow. The crystal split into pieces, and our hearts split with it. The surrounding crystals also split, shards flying everywhere.

The chamber was plunged into darkness, and – at least for the time being – *Cana Dei* released its grip on our souls.

❈ 13 ❈

AFTER DARK

The darkness lingered. The odours of sulphur and rotten vegetable juice melded with those of sweat, fear, and perfume. The rotten taste of bile cloyed in the back of my throat, and the cold sweat underneath my fur caused my skin to itch. Feet began to shuffle, students began to speak, the teachers started to relay their instructions for everyone to remain calm.

"*Salanraja,*" I said. "*Salanraja, can you hear me?*"

I'd realised that throughout the entire time *Cana Dei* had been showing us Seramina's vision that my dragon had been absent from my mind.

"*Ben,*" she said. "*Gracious demons, I heard what happened. How is it possible? Things are much more dire than we thought.*"

"*Maybe you can come in and get us.*"

"*No ... Farago, Flue, and Plishk have given us all instructions. Don't worry, it's under control. Just follow any*" *instructions you're given and we'll be back in the air in no time."*

"But the crystal, Salanraja. Our crystal. Will we ever hear its voice again?"

"I don't know … Just have hope, okay? Stay strong …"

"I wish I could, Salanraja. But everything seems to be changing for the worse."

To that, Salanraja remained silent. I guess there wasn't much she could say, and she probably was dealing with worries of her own. I heard Aleam's croaky voice within the darkness.

"My team, please gather. I need to check you're all here."

I edged closer to the voice, taking extra care not to slide over the wet earth. It didn't feel like it would be easy to get a claw-hold on, and some of the drops from the ledge had looked quite steep.

"Seramina, Seramina, are you here?"

There was a momentary pause, and for a while I'd half expected Seramina to have slipped away. The vision had shown her as a hermit, fighting the warlocks alone. She couldn't escape destiny, so why not embrace it?

"I'm here," Seramina said, after a moment, her voice clearly strained. "I'm okay …"

"Good … Ange?"

"Present," Ange said.

"Esme."

"Here." She said it in the human language.

"Ta'ra."

"Yes."

"Ben."

"Yes."

"Max ..."

"Wargs! Wargs! Too many evil wargs!"

The first sign of illumination emerged through the darkness. At first, it looked like it was coming from strange candles floating in the chamber beneath us. It wasn't long until I realised that the source of the light was glowing unicorn horns, sending swirling patterns across the magical creatures' manes.

I detected a whiff of camphor, and then Driar Yila lit the first torch using a plain old match. She used her torch to light one in Driar Brigel's hand, and then more torches were being lit and passed out to each of the teachers. I could feel the heat coming off Aleam's. A few flames dripped at my feet and then guttered out.

Despite everyone being scared to the point of having goosebumps, there was no panic. We filtered out of the chamber one group at a time, through the passageway and into the adjoining chamber. This was much smaller, but thank the whiskers it had working crystals in it, providing light and again showing visions of the future. Though these were a little small to make out the details, no crystal displayed the terrifying scene in which Seramina would destroy the worlds, and for that I was thankful.

Aleam, who for the last year or so had served as Seramina's guardian, stood just in front of the teenager, as if to shelter her from the glances she was getting from the students. They kept pointing at her and gossiping about who knows what in hushed murmurs.

Now the truth was out. Only a select number of us had previously known about this prophecy; Seramina was destined to battle the warlocks and ultimately destroy the worlds. Prophecies foretold by the crystals didn't always come true, admittedly – they only showed one of many possibilities.

But *Cana Dei* had revealed this threat before destroying the Great Crystal that was meant to make everything okay again. It had done so for a reason, implying Seramina was somehow an agent of the dark force.

It was no secret that Seramina was the deceased warlock Astravar's daughter, nor that Seramina had known how to use dark magic from a very early age. Once, during a battle at the Altar of Lore against the warlocks, *Cana Dei* had almost taken control of her soul. But, working together with us, Esme had managed to summon Bastet, who after defeating the massive demon snake Apopis had helped to save her. Then, after we'd gained white magic, just before we'd defeated the evil Warlock Prince Arran, I'd thought she would never turn back to the darkness again.

Alas while we'd been strengthening, clearly so too had *Cana Dei*. Now it had grown more powerful than ever.

If we let it take control of Seramina, we'd lose any

chance we had of defeating it. From the way Seramina stood staring at the absent spot where the Great Crystal had been, it was clear that she feared her destiny more than anyone else.

A CONVERSATION

The Council of Three and Alliander had gone ahead of us, but it didn't take us long to catch up with them. Actually our team, led by the venerable Driar Aleam, was one of the first to reach the safety of the lit cavern. Though *Cana Dei* had found its way into the Great Crystal, it hadn't taken the other crystals in the Versta Caverns. Or if it had, it hadn't found a way to destroy them. That was a good thing.

The Council of Three and the White Mage captain stood at a cloistered off section of the chamber in an alcove, speaking in hushed voices. Tanni, Alliander's unicorn, stayed close to her, and he kept turning his head from side to side as if looking out for any danger. We now seemed safe; the caverns now had a regular earthy cave smell, and I couldn't detect a whiff of rotten vegetable juice.

I sat on the cold wet floor between Ta'ra and Esme, and the three of us had our ears turned towards the conversation. Humans always forgot how good we cats were at hearing, and our ability to understand their language made eavesdropping easy.

"I thought you said that you had the girl under control," Alliander said.

"We do have her under control," Great Driar Yila replied. "The vision's always been the same, but we've all been watching the girl closely. And we've been giving her extra tuition, as King Garmin formally advised."

"And who's *we*?" asked Alliander.

"That's us," Driar Brigel said. "Yila, Lonamm, and myself. As well as Driar Aleam, of course. He's been watching over her for a long time."

Alliander scoffed. "You mean, Aleam the former warlock?"

"He never became a warlock," Driar Lonamm said. "You know full well since that awful day the warlocks turned on us, Aleam has done nothing but show full loyalty to king and country."

"Yet we keep returning to the same place," Alliander said. "The same vision, where Initiate Seramina destroys everything. No matter how much we've tried to change it, the outcome is always the same."

I looked at Esme, who blinked at me innocently. I hadn't realised that the White Mages knew the exact details of the prophecy.

"What are you proposing?" Driar Yila asked, and though I couldn't see her eyes, I'd seen her hawk-like stare enough times to know exactly how she was looking at Alliander. "I hope you're not suggesting ..."

"Gracious demons, no ... What do you take me for? You know it is against the Code of the White to allow any harm to come to a minor. But that doesn't mean we can't keep her under strict guard."

Driar Yila coughed. "We are quite capable—"

Alliander held up her hand and showed Driar Yila her palm. "I'm sorry, Great Driar Yila, and all of you, really. Though I respect the service that the Council of Three has done for this country, this time I need to impose Article Five-Two of the ancient Magna Dictate, our code of law."

"*Oh no,*" Salanraja said in my head. "*Not Article Five-Two.*"

"*What the whiskers is Article Five-Two?*"

"*You'll find out, just listen ...*"

"*I was—*"

I let Alliander's voice cut off my thoughts, because her words came out as clear as a bowl of water. "From this day on until we resolve this conflict with *Cana Dei,*" she said. "Dragonsbond Academy is under martial law."

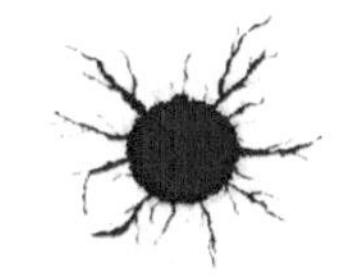

INTERLUDE
CANA DEI

Well, well, didn't we cause quite the commotion? We work so well as a team, don't you think? Oh yes, you think it was all my doing, but if it weren't for your existence, my dear Seramina, then the vision wouldn't exist in the first place. All it takes is one spectacular chunk of rock – a single crystal – to crumble into sand, and everything changes.

Thus the seed of fear is placed, and our marvellous plans are going swimmingly. There is no better way to win a war than to complete obliterate all hope in your opponent. Then, when the two of you finally clash, you hardly need to fight at all.

Now fly home, Seramina. Let your dragon, who has pledged loyalty to you for his whole life, bear you upon his back. I'm sorry to say that you may not be able to keep your bond with him when we're finished, because I can't imagine a creature so noble and pure succumbing to my will. But you must, my dear child. Together, I promise, we can change the worlds.

Oh, and I watch you through the crystal of your staff. I'm surprised the White Mage captain hasn't confiscated it like she did that time before. But even if she did, I can watch you from that dark place in your mind.

You feel guilty now, I know. Yet perhaps *guilt* is too weak a word. You feel ashamed, and so you should, Seramina. Because it is shameful to live in such a sorry world. Just because you're younger than them, doesn't mean that people can control you.

But you are more powerful than any of them. When you have finally learned what I have to teach you, you will be able to shatter walls with a snap of your fingers. You will stamp your feet against the earth and the shining towers of Cimlean City will come crumbling down. You shall sit upon the king's very throne, and you will sit there long enough until you realise it doesn't hold any power whatsoever.

For the power is within you, dear Seramina. You *can* control it all.

And trust me, you will, but not without my help. You will always be sitting at my side.

AND NOW IN THE BLINK OF AN EYE I SEE YOU, Ammit, the glow from the burning brimstone in the seas that surround your cliff gleaming off your skin. You are serving me well.

Are my armies ready? Yes, I can see them through your very own glowing eyes. Thousands upon thousands of demons, a menagerie of beasts; each one of them shall serve in the battle.

And each shall serve in the best of all possible ways. Armies amassing, more demons across the rocky climes of the Seventh Dimension than most even realise exist. I see them crawling out of the lava. I see them all.

Here, a demon gazelle that can rain down terror in a mighty leap. There, a demon hippopotamus – it is the one whom Dragoncat fears the most. And over there in the distance, the mighty demon mammoth, with enough power in your tusks and shoulders to topple towers. Such a mighty army indeed ...

I am proud of you, Ammit, and soon your time shall come.

Meanwhile ... oh my poor dear fated Lasinta. Why do you still resist the pull of *Cana Dei*? You fabled 'warlocks' are all the same. You dance the precipice between power and darkness every day, and you have the arrogance to believe you will never fall.

And you only need to fall once, Lasinta. It only takes one slip.

I'm still unsure whether I will finally take you as my servant or toss you away. I guess destiny will dictate that, won't it? The destiny that you've been avoiding for so long.

For now, I see you've amassed a powerful army of your own. I can see them from the crystal of your staff, because a user of the darkest force in all the worlds cannot hide from the vision of said force. Together we watch from the height of the seven-spoked platform on top of the Tower of the Warlocks.

Below us the beautiful purple clouds – *my* creation. And row upon row of magical creatures – golems, manipulators, bone dragons – all of them powered by crystal hearts – *my* magic.

You plan to charge. If you can destroy Seramina before she even has a chance to fulfil the prophecy, then it will never have to come to pass.

It's such a wonderful plan ...

Such a foolish plan ...

So go on, Lasinta. Challenge destiny. I dare you ... Because fate has already decided the outcome. Inevitably, your actions *will* change the worlds.

❦ 15 ❧

ANOTHER TRAITOR

Fire burning all around me, searing my fur and itching at my skin. Fear spiking my heart, palpitating in irregular rhythms. For amongst the mica cliffs of the seventh dimension, beneath towering shards of obsidian that pierce the red, sulphuric sky, lay an army. Demons of all imaginable kinds stacked like dominoes. In front of them, a recognisable face – the jaws of a crocodile, the paws of a lion, and the hindquarters of a hippopotamus.

Ammit was ready to conquer. I could see it in the fires inside the depths of her burning eyes. *Cana Dei's* voice roared like thunder across the sky.

"This is the future, Dragoncat."

Suddenly Ammit clicked her mighty jaws together, and she tossed her snout upwards. Out came her command, bellowing yet incomprehensible. A sheet of red and darkness spread across the ground beneath the burning army, and then came the light, and a portal opened, and then—

The smell of mutton sausages. The crackle of a camp-fire outside. It was enough to draw me back into the real world, because this Bengal was so hungry. *Cana Dei* might have temporarily taken control of my mind, but it couldn't control my tummy.

I was lying on the bench in Aleam's workshop, a sliver of light from the half-moon shining in through the window. The old man stood at his alembic, adding a few drops of green liquid to some yellow fluid already bubbling away inside the apparatus. A torch hanging over the apparatus provided some additional but sparse light. Aleam didn't notice me stir, nor did he see me drop down onto the floor.

"*Ben, you've awoken,*" Salanraja said.

"*I smell mutton sausages. Someone's cooking.*"

I was already stalking out through the open gap between Aleam's door and its frame. I would have moved faster, but my muscles were weak from sleep. Perhaps *Cana Dei* had taken over my legs, because they seemed to be telling me I didn't need food. But my stomach had a different opinion about that.

"*Outside ...*" Salanraja continued. "*The Council of Three wanted to do something to cheer you up. But your dream ... That was—*"

"*It was nothing! Nothing that cannot wait. I need to eat, Salanraja. Can you not hear how my tummy was rumbling all the way home? And mutton sausages – we're*" *always meant to stop off and have mutton sausages on the way."*

"I don't think Alliander would have allowed that," Salanraja said.

"I'm surprised she's even allowing a feast. It's just not Alliander's style."

"I guess she wants to butter you all up before establishing her iron rule of martial law. Or maybe she just wants to show that she has no enmity with anyone save Seramina."

"*Seramina …*" I said. I felt really bad about her, and I wished there was something I could do. If I hadn't encouraged her to commune with *Cana Dei* before, maybe none of this would have happened. But then, if she were destined to destroy the worlds, was there anything any of us could do to stop it?

Right in the centre of the bailey, not far from the fountain, raged a bonfire. Its flames towered high, dancing rhythmically, sending embers upwards. These floated like fairies into a dark and bleak sky.

The students had set up a turnspit, with an oversized hamster wheel turning a network of sausages roasting over the fire. The Sussex spaniel, Max, ran on the wheel, and he did so while panting happily. Esme and Ta'ra sat on either side of him, both staring at the dog as if they thought him a gullible idiot. But he had a good pile of cooked sausages lined up next to him, guarded by a White Mage. When he was done with his exercise he would certainly eat well.

Students stood around the fire, watching the flames

lick lazily at the darkness above. Unicorns kept click-clacking their hooves, cantering around as they also waited for food. Apparently, unicorns ate meat too – unlike their brethren the horses, they weren't vegetarians. From the amount of meat toasting over the fire, I could see there would be plenty to go around.

I went to find a human who could get me some sausages, ignoring Rine and Bellari cuddling up on a bench by the fire, much too close to each other for my comfort. Instead, I tried to detect the scent of snowdrop perfume. I wanted to have a good chat with Seramina. I wanted her to know that whatever happened, I was on her side.

After all, I had started to make different plans for my retirement. I didn't need to settle down in a country cottage with Rine and Ange anymore. Seramina and Ange would be enough, good friends living together. Ange could use her leaf magic to create food for the chickens and cows and sheep that would eventually end up in my tummy. And Seramina – she could look after us all. She could forget about magic completely and become the kind, cat-loving woman she was destined to be.

I really didn't believe that she was fated to destroy the worlds. That was just *Cana Dei* trying to trick us.

Instead of finding Seramina, I latched on to Ange's scent of catnip. She was sitting on a bench speaking to Bellari's ex-boyfriend Kamino, who wore a vest and had big muscles and even bigger feet. She was laughing and Kamino was laughing too, as they both ate from vellum plates resting on their laps.

I rubbed against Ange's calf to get her attention, and I jumped up onto the bench between her and Kamino. Though I didn't think Ange needed Rine, I didn't particularly like her flirting with other boys either. Ange no longer wore her yellow shoulder pads that denoted her as a prefect, and as I glanced around, I noticed that none of the prefects here did – not even Bellari. Whatever authority they'd had, had been removed.

"Well, well," Kamino said, looking down at me. "If it isn't Bellari's nemesis."

"Don't call him that," Ange said, punching Kamino's shoulder. "Ben's a very nice Bengal, aren't you, Ben?" She tickled me under the chin.

"Descendant of the great Asian leopard cat—" I said.

"—and the mighty George," Ange butted in, and then she giggled.

Really, I didn't get what was so funny. She seemed giddy, and I really hoped it wasn't because of this boy who had feet large enough for a career in clowning. Not trusting anything with big feet was a code we cats lived by, and it had served us well for a long time.

"Honestly, I don't get why he's so full of himself," Kamino said with a shrug. "I mean he's a cat, and yeah, he can use magic. But that doesn't make him more special than any of us, now, does it?"

I snapped my head around towards him, and I bared my teeth, letting out a brief hiss. "I'll have you know that I'm the dragon rider who defeated Astravar."

"Really?" Kamino asked. "Is that true? Because I heard it was the Cat Sidhe. She used her fairy magic to save you from being fried by Astravar's magic." He pointed a fork towards Ta'ra, who was now sleeping by the fire, a half-eaten sausage underneath her paw.

"She helped," I said. "But I delivered the final blow with my staff that knocked him off his aeriosaur mount."

"And yet you wouldn't have done it without her fairy magic, I hear. If she hadn't cast such a powerful spell, the warlock would have eaten you alive."

"Oh, shut up!"

"Oh okay, then, if you insist," he said with a grin.

But I wasn't liking this. "Ange … What are you doing with this boy? He's repulsive."

Ange's expression turned sour. "He's …" she looked at him, then back down at me with an angry frown. "Look, are you really going to do this now, Ben? Can't I just have some time to enjoy myself with my new friend here?"

"I only wanted to come over and ask if you can give me some food. I'm hungry, and you know I can't get it for myself."

"Here, you can have this …" She tossed the plate with the sausage on it from her lap onto the floor. She took her hand away from my chin and instead placed in on Kamino's arm. "We can share, can't we Kamino?"

His gaze met hers. "Sure we can."

It was so sickening to watch that I decided to leave the two of them alone. At that moment I decided I didn't need Ange in my retirement plans either. I slinked off the bench to enjoy some mutton in peace.

16

ESTABLISHING ORDER

I'd managed to get halfway through my sausage, eating it slowly and savouring the delight of the way the fatty meat settled on my tongue, when Captain Alliander decided to ruin the moment for us. I had only just worked out by eavesdropping on snippets of students' conversations that Seramina was locked in the castle's gatehouse. Alliander had posted five mounted White Mages at the base of the tower, and ordered two of the castle guards to stand by her door at all times. She had also warded the entrance and the arrow slits with powerful white magic to prevent Seramina's escape. To make matters worse, Alliander had confiscated her staff and had it locked away in a secure location that she wouldn't reveal to anyone.

Even if she apparently was the most powerful mage alive, Seramina had no chance of getting out of her prison without her staff. At the same time, I didn't see any sign of anyone delivering food up to her. I really hoped that Alliander didn't plan to starve her in the tower.

Alliander clapped her hands together loudly, and then she screamed out at the top of her lungs, "Okay, it's time for silence now!"

Unlike the Great Driars at the assembly earlier that day, no one dared challenge the Captain of the White Guard's authority. Everyone's voices cut off as if she had flicked a light switch to plunge the bailey into darkness. Heads snapped around to stare at her, and those seated quickly shifted themselves off their benches.

Captain Alliander had a terrible reputation for enacting severe punishments at the School of the White, where she trained White Mages when she wasn't on active duty. I'd heard stories of how she liked to line students up in trains, each with their two hands on the shoulders of the student in front. Then, as a single row, they'd all have to perform squats at once, whilst reciting the exact nature of the crime that they'd committed, in the exact words that Alliander dictated to them.

This, of course, was hard to imagine as a cat. I'd heard rumours that after enough squats, the pain in their legs was excruciating for the students. Even worse, the White Mages often said, was the humiliation.

Alliander scanned the space around her, head held high as if appreciating the silence. For a moment all that could be heard was the crackle of the fire, the sizzling of the sausages, and the distant hoot of an owl.

"Good," she said, an air of haughtiness in her voice that reminded me of her stepbrother, the evil, now vanquished, and unlamented Warlock Prince, Arran. "I have to say I'm astounded. Students at the School of the White tell me what rogues you dragon riders are, but today you seem much more disciplined than I expected. Discipline, I hope you all agree, is incredibly important within the king's ranks. Particularly in such troubled times."

I looked around for the Council of Three, or any of the Driars who in fact usually taught in the academy. None of them was to be seen, probably locked within the Keep Tower whilst the White Mages and their unicorns kept things running outside. But I could see the moonlight glinting off the armour of the regular castle guards on the parapets.

"I'm going to be blunt with you," Alliander continued. "The vision that we saw within the Versta Caverns doesn't look good at all. We've never seen so many crystals shatter all at once like that, even when attacked by dark magic. The teenager you know as Seramina is under strict martial guard. No one is to speak to her, and my White Mages at her door have been instructed to treat anyone trying to do so with extreme prejudice. Any attempt to enter her current quarters, or to bring her anything, will be severely punished. All the staff at Dragonsbond Academy have been ordered to report any malevolent behaviour directly to me. This is the same for any of you, and if you happen to notice anything suspicious, let's just say any useful information that you provide will serve you well in your future career."

All this was getting quite boring – not that anything

Alliander said was ever interesting in the first place. I took another bite from the sausage, delighting in the way that the juices spilled over my tongue.

"*Enjoying that, Ben?*" said a voice in my head, and hearing it sent up the hackles on the back of my neck.

The voice didn't belong to Salanraja, nor did it belong to *Cana Dei*. It wasn't the voice of my crystal that I hadn't heard for months. It didn't belong to Bastet, the Oracle Fairy, or Brigid either – immortals who had all spoken inside my mind at one point or another. Instead, the voice was that of Seramina, and I'd never before let her in. Which meant one of two things – either I was hearing things, or she'd decided to buy into the whole telepathy thing, as if having a dragon in your head all the time weren't enough.

"*Come on,*" she said. "*You know I'm a mind mage, and so I've always been able to do this. It's nothing unusual.*"

"*What do you mean nothing unusual?*" I asked. "*Back home, the old Ragamuffin used to tell us that hearing voices in your head was the first sign of madness. The second sign was chasing your own tail for hours on end. And humans always used to confuse the issue by using a laser beam to make you perform that very act, and they always found it hysterical.*"

"*What's a laser?*"

"*A laser, you know – light amplification by stimulated emission of radiation.*" Sometimes, in this dimension, having the gift to be able to speak all languages could make me sound really smart.

"*Oh, you mean a magelight? Anyway, whatever you call it, I'm, sure your old Ragamuffin was talking about imagined voices. Now I'm speaking to you for real.*"

"*But how do I know it's you? It could be* Cana Dei *playing tricks inside my head.*"

"*Just, Ben ... Listen out for me from the guard tower. I'm just about to call out 'the owl only hoots between the hours of dusk and dawn.' Think of it as a code phrase.*"

I turned my ears towards the guard tower, and indeed she screamed it out. Probably the humans couldn't hear it with Captain Alliander rabbiting on about the importance of martial law to protect the kingdom, and the various times it had been enforced throughout Illumine Kingdom's history.

But the guard outside her door certainly heard it, and he screamed back for her to shut up because he was trying to concentrate.

"*Okay, so it is you,*" I said. "*But if you've been able to talk all this time inside my mind, why only use the ability now?*"

"*Well, it's a bit intrusive, don't you think? Still, I need your help. Ben, this is important.*"

"*You know, Alliander has already promised severe punishments if I'm found doing anything for you, including communicating with you.*"

"*Which is why I'm not using White Magic to do this.*"

"*So you're continuing to use* Cana Dei. *You know the risks. Wait, didn't Alliander confiscate your staff?*"

"*I don't need my staff anymore, Ben. I can forge a new one out of thin air if I want.*"

"You're kidding," I said. I remembered the ordeal that I'd had to go through to get my own staff. I'd had to fight three of my ancestors, the great Asian leopard cats, to get it. *"Wait a minute, how did you know that Alliander said all this? You're much too far away to hear what she's saying, and you don't have a cat's spectacular hearing."*

"I've been listening inside your mind," she replied sheepishly.

Without even thinking about it, I let a low-pitched growl come out of my throat. A student standing nearby looked at me with a sneer, then shook her head and turned back towards Alliander. From the walls a crow croaked, and the wind cried out in a loud howl, kicking up an eddy of dust on the parapets. A mounted female White Mage stationed just below the wall looked upwards and watched the crow fly overhead. The staff in her hand glowed white for a moment, making her cloak seem to glow.

"Great, another creature invading my privacy," I said to Seramina. *"Why can't you telepaths just give this poor Bengal time to be alone with his thoughts?"*

I waited for an objection from Salanraja, but none came.

"Look Ben," Seramina continued, *"I'm sorry, but I don't have time for this.* Cana Dei *has shown me something ... Lasinta and the other warlocks are moving towards Dragonsbond Academy as I speak. She's bringing an army with her."*

"What? Why? Who's the target?"

"They're coming to dispose of me, Ben. But I'm sure she

won't mind if she wiped out some of her other enemies in the process too."

"Whiskers," I said. *"Are you sure?"*

"I know enough about destiny magic to know when the possible threads of the future are converging towards a single point. This is about to happen, Ben. I'm certain."

"And how long have we got until the armies arrive?"

"I don't know, a day or two, max. The warlocks will meet with very little resistance at the Great Barrier on the way. Apparently Alliander has called back her guards from there to help fortify her position at Dragonsbond Academy. They seem to think that I'm more of a threat than the warlocks."

"This isn't good," I said.

"It isn't ... You know what will happen if I meet her, Ben. You've seen the visions too. We have to do whatever we can to prevent that."

I knew exactly what she meant, and I knew that she'd need help breaking out and getting away as far as possible. But first, I'd have to work out who my allies were. Given how often Seramina was communing with *Cana Dei*, I wasn't sure I could trust her as an ally either.

"Just give me a night to work it out," I said. *"I'll see what I can do."*

17

ALLIES

Alliander had started detailing a list of punishments she would enact if anyone were found to be conspiring with Seramina, which made the infamous squatting routine seem minor. Being sent to the Crystal Mountains in just a shirt and breeches and doing labour under the great dragon trainer Matharon's supervision in the freezing cold. Then, through use of White Magic, having your bond with your dragon broken for a week – which apparently caused students to roll around on the floor in fits of sobbing for the entire duration. Then, for a whole day, entering a magically created simulation that made your mind think that you were falling into a bottomless well without anything to catch you. And after that, not being allowed to ride a dragon in service of the king ever again.

She'd made the consequences sound so severe that I knew I didn't have a chance of getting a regular student to aid me in breaking Seramina out. Besides, Rine was too besotted with Bellari, and Ange had interests of her own, though I couldn't work out if she was truly interested in Kamino or just trying to make Rine jealous. Max was far too loyal. The old man Aleam was out of reach. There was Esme, of course, but if she discovered how much Seramina had been communing with *Cana Dei*, she'd run screaming for Alliander to place extra wards on her cell.

That left only one option – my old and faithful *companion*, Ta'ra. I couldn't see her by the campfire, so instead I went to seek her out by scent. I found her lying underneath the bailey's fountain – one of my favourite hiding places that she'd also seemed to have adopted. The best places for cats are those not easily accessible to humans, which is why a lot of cats prefer to hide under beds and bushes rather than beneath a simple coffee table.

Tara had sequestered away a mutton sausage, and she was munching on it like a naturally born carnivore. I was proud to see that. We'd been through a period when I was training her to be a cat that she'd refused to eat meat. She'd pointed out that all fairies were vegetarians and, given she used to be a fairy, she'd wanted to stick to her traditions. Eventually she'd needed to give in to her cravings. A cat's biology just can't survive on all the weird stuff that humans like to consume.

It was cold underneath the fountain. The narrow space there, being so low, failed to trap the heat of the fire. The flagstones had even managed to gather some frost. But still, with everything going on, it seemed a much more comfortable spot than anywhere else.

"I wondered when you'd come to seek me out, Ben," Ta'ra said, and she pushed her wet nose against mine. "Your other *companion* Esme is so interested in what Alliander has to say that I thought this would be a good opportunity to spend some alone time with you."

"Oh, I'm sure we'll have plenty of time for that," I said.

"We will, will we?" Ta'ra said, and a speck of moonlight glinted off her green eyes. She pushed her nose up to me again. "You know, I think we could make this martial law situation kind of fun."

"I think so too," I said. "Because I've got a grand adventure planned."

"Do you?" Ta'ra cocked her head demurely. "Why, what are you planning?"

I stopped to take a deep breath. I wasn't entirely sure Ta'ra was going to go for this. But for Seramina's sake, I had to try ...

"We're going to rescue Seramina."

The expression on Ta'ra's face fell. For a moment, she looked as if I'd stolen her mackerel – which I'd never actually done despite being accused of it several times. She glared daggers at me and then looked sharply away.

"Ben, have you been listening to anything that Captain Alliander has been saying? She's not one to be messed with, you know. Her reputation for cruelty has carried over even into the Faerie Realm."

"I heard exactly what she said. But Ta'ra, there's more going on than you think there is."

I told her everything. How I'd caught Seramina communing with *Cana Dei*, and how she'd seen that vision just before our failed attempt to retrieve the Great Crystal. My dreams about Ammit building an army, and how Seramina had dropped into my mind and told me that Lasinta was already on the march. I made it clear that we couldn't let Seramina face the warlocks in battle like that. Last time she had done that, she'd ended up summoning a whole stream of the all-devouring dark mist of *Cana Dei* into this world, which had almost annihilated us all. Ta'ra hadn't been present during that conflict, and so she watched me with intent as I told the story, as if she were learning something new.

"So how we going to free her?" Ta'ra asked after I'd finished.

"Well, if you can distract the guards for long enough, maybe I'll be able to use my magic to destroy the wards."

Ta'ra laughed in a very cat-like, whining way. It was very unlike a she-cat, but I decided it was better not to point that out.

"You're not that powerful, Ben," she said. "There's no way that you could destroy Alliander's wards. And then just think what she might do to you. She'll turn you into a mouse and have the cats of the cattery chasing you across the bailey."

I growled at her – I really didn't like being told about my flaws. There was a pause, then from nearby there came a rustle of fur.

"I know exactly what you should do," Esme said.

Both Ta'ra and I turned our heads sharply, and I ended up banging mine on one of the support stones of the fountain. Esme had sneakily found her way over to us, and she'd been spying just inches from our position. I hadn't heard her approach, let alone smelled her. But then there was so much meat cooking, it was hard to focus my nose on anything else.

"Esme," I said, "if you say a word—"

"I think you've forgotten whose side I'm on," she said. "Fortunately for you, your dragon has been listening within your head, and reported your stupid plans to Kada who passed them directly on to me."

"*Salanraja!*" I said inside my mind. "*I wondered why you were so silent ... and you're meant to be on* my *side.*"

"*I just don't want you to go ahead and do anything rash, Bengie. It might have helped if you'd discussed it with me first. But you always go planning things on your own ...*"

She continued to drone on with a pointless lecture, but I ignored her, because Esme was still speaking.

"Look," the Abyssinian said, "although I wish you'd spoken to me about Seramina's secret tryst with *Cana Dei* – especially since I'm the one who's been teaching you how to ward it off – I also agree that we need to get Seramina away from here, despite the potential consequences."

"I thought you said that you didn't want me doing anything stupid," I objected.

"Yes, your plan was stupid," Esme said.

"Agreed," Ta'ra put in – the first time in days she'd actually taken the Abyssinian's side on anything.

"Fine, so what do you propose?" I asked.

"We're going to enlist the help of the cats in the cattery," Esme said. "I hear that an old friend of ours has recently been brought in here, and he doesn't like being there at all."

"You mean we're going to break them out?"

"Yes, we're going to break them out."

"I like it," I said.

And I could see from the glint in Ta'ra's eyes that she did too.

18

THE HATCH

We waited for the martial-law food party to end before we attempted the breakout. By this time the cloud cover had broken and a half-moon had risen high in the sky. Even though I'd eaten, the smell of mutton lingered, confusing my brain and making my tummy rumble continuously. It blended with the remnants of burned charcoal, and very faintly I could often detect a whiff of rotten vegetable juice.

Ta'ra, Esme, and I had remained under the fountain all this time. No one seemed to notice us missing. Rather, after the students were corralled and shepherded back to their rooms, we waited silently, listening to the conversations between Alliander and her guards.

Carmista was there, Alliander's trusted White Mage lieutenant, whom we'd had run-ins with before. She'd been out scouting on her unicorn, and she reported sightings of wargs outside the Willowed Woods to the north. Clearly they'd ignored the threat posed by Max and me the other day, and had decided to emerge again.

"There's a whole army of them," Carmista said. "And more and more seem to be gathering."

"But wargs never leave the Willowed Woods," Alliander objected. "Why come out now?"

"Perhaps they're planning to charge, ma'am. If enough of them flock together, we might have quite a battle on our hands."

"We'll break them up long before that happens. Redeploy scouts on their perimeter to keep an eye on them."

"Affirmative, ma'am."

Carmista saluted, then she and her unicorn trotted off towards the gate. The portcullis creaked open to let her out, and the drawbridge as it lowered made that horrible clanking sound that drawbridges make.

"*That doesn't sound good,*" Salanraja said inside my mind. "*If Seramina's right about the warlocks approaching from the south, then the wargs must be a decoy.*"

"*And presumably the warlocks control the wargs,*" I replied. "*How do they manage to do so from such a distance?*"

"*Gracious demons. Did you pay attention in any of your 'Nature of Dark Magic' lessons, Bengie? The wargs don't answer to the warlocks. They answer to* Cana Dei.*"

"*That's even worse,*" I said with a shudder. Or, in all honesty, I felt that it was worse, but I didn't quite understand why.

"*Precisely,*" Salanraja said. "*Lasinta is trying to resist*

Cana Dei, *so she wants to work with it as little as possible. But* Cana Dei *must have a reason for drawing out the wargs. I'm guessing it wants to increase the chance that Seramina and the warlocks meet."*

"We can't tell anyone, Salanraja." I said. "If Alliander realises we're about to break Seramina out she'll punish us severely. Something tells me that she has something special in mind for us cats, because cats can't physically do squats like humans can."

"She'll probably make you eat regular cat food."

"That's what I'm dreading. I can't think of anything worse…"

While I was speaking to Salanraja inside my head, Esme, Ta'ra and I sat underneath the fountain staring at the white suede shoes Alliander wore on her feet. I guessed the other two cats were having conversations with their dragons too, because the three of us remained silent. Alliander lingered a moment then marched off towards the keep tower, the steel soles at the bottom of her low heels clinking against the flagstones.

"So it's time, I guess," I said.

"Never a better opportunity," Esme said. "Come on, Ben … Ta'ra."

She sprinted off across the bailey, her alabaster fur seeming to shimmer under the moonlight.

"So eager," Ta'ra said.

"Well, I guess she's right," I said. "We haven't got much time."

I pulled myself out from under the fountain and followed Esme over to the oak hardwood hatch that opened into the cattery. Two male White Guards in their white robes sat on their unicorns by the archway that led out from the bailey into the inner courtyard beneath the keep tower. Their gazes didn't seem focused on the cattery, but rather on the guardhouse within which Seramina was safely locked. Esme had concealed herself far enough into the shadows by this point as to not be visible in the moonlight, so I'm not sure they realised we were here. Or, if they did, they didn't seem to be paying us any heed.

A heavy cast iron chain kept the hatch sealed shut, and from behind it I could hear the cries of hundreds of cats miaowing for food and comfort. Usually they'd be let out at this time of night to stalk the castle grounds and hunt the rats and other vermin. But with this new martial law, the curfew also seemed to apply to the cats.

"It's terrible for them to be locked up like that," I said. "I've never liked it."

"I've told you before," Esme replied, "it's a veritable palace in there compared to the rest of the world."

"Yeah, I remember you saying that it's absolute luxury."

I examined the massive heavy padlock that fastened the chain. It was cold and smelled of rust, but despite that it seemed pretty sturdy. More miaows came from below, as if the cats could smell us. But that trapdoor looked like it wouldn't let anything through – not even scent. It made me wonder where the cattery got its ventilation from.

"The White Mages locked this," Esme said.

"Alliander didn't want any students sneaking through the underground passageways."

"So how are we going to get inside?" I asked.

"I presumed that you were going to use magic," Ta'ra said. "Wasn't that the plan all along?"

"Yes, of course we're going to use magic," Esme said, licking her paw.

She glanced at the two White Guards. One had a coin in her hand that seemed to glow as she flicked it up into the air and caught it again. Clearly, any spell we cast would draw their attention, unless we found a way of masking it first.

"So you'll cast the glamour, and I'll break the lock?" I asked.

Esme brushed up next to me and she pushed her nose to the lock, sniffing it. "I'm afraid this lock is warded with strong White Magic. Do you think you can cast a strong enough glamour to fool those mages, Ben?"

I looked at them, then I sniffed the air as a whiff of unicorn came over, strangely tainted with White Magic. One of the unicorns, I noticed, seemed to have its beady yellow eye looking directly at me.

"I don't think so," I said.

"Nor do I," Esme said. She turned to Ta'ra. "Okay, time for Plan B. I want you two to distract the guards while I break the lock."

The hackles shot up immediately on Ta'ra's back. She hissed, displaying her sharp teeth. "I thought you said I wasn't going to have to do any distracting?"

"Well," Esme said. "It looks like we don't have any choice. Just think – we're doing this for Seramina."

Ta'ra looked at me, her eyes wide. They told me exactly what my heart told me, beating in turbo. Esme was planning to break the cats out, then free Seramina, leaving Ta'ra and me to be captured by the White Mages. Meanwhile, we'd be the ones who got punished.

A croaky voice came from above us, cutting off my train of thought. In the darkness, a roughly humanoid shadow seemed to shimmer. "And why don't you just use the key?"

The old man, Aleam, stepped out of the glamour that he'd been casting into the void, a heavy brass key in his hand.

In his other hand he held his staff. The crystal on the top of it glowed with the pure whiteness of glamour magic, semi-transparent streams running off from it in a loose dome towards the ground. The White Mages didn't seem to have noticed any disturbance, one continually focusing on his magical coin and the other staring out into the night. The unicorn that had been watching me with intent had also seemed to lose interest, now chewing on a tuft of grass that stuck out from between the flagstones.

Aleam bent down and unlocked the padlock. He was careful as he unravelled the chain, treating it as if it were a poisonous snake, so as not to make any noise. A whiff of catness came from behind the hatch when Aleam opened it, but the cats themselves had stopped meowing.

It was dark behind the trapdoor, but Aleam didn't

make any move to light a torch. Rather he turned back to us, then whispered, "Come on. I'll explain everything when we're inside."

He descended into the darkness. We three cats followed him. Behind us, the trapdoor closed as if powered by a magic of its own, sealing us inside.

19

FELINE ALLIANCE

Fortunately, we cats are well equipped for finding our way through darkness. Humans have been so impressed by this ability throughout history that they've perpetuated the rumour that we can see in the dark. This isn't technically true.

Indeed, we have eyes well suited for seeing in dim light, but within the darkest of darkness, we have to rely on our other senses. It's just that unlike those of humans, these senses are finely attuned. We have whiskers on our paws to feel our way, can sense vibrations in the ground, and of course we have our delicate senses of smell and hearing.

So, after the trapdoor closed behind us in the basement underneath the castle, we had to use our noses to follow him through the dark and down the staircase. Still, he seemed to also navigate well, as if he knew the location of every single step.

There came a spark followed by the smell of burning

phosphorus. The light on the match in Aleam's hand lit his face, showing the caverns between his wrinkles. He set it to a torch on the wall, and soon the chamber filled with light.

Cats' eyes all around us reflected the torchlight – shining gems of emerald and gold and topaz. There was now enough light to see the entire cattery, and I gazed at it with unexpected awe. Esme had been right – this wasn't a prison at all. Nor was it filled with cages everywhere, as the cattery I'd visited had been back home in South Wales. Instead, the hatch led to an underground network of tunnels spanning off from one large, cavernous chamber in a dozen or so directions. It looked like the whole place had been dug out by supersized ants.

Now, back in my home in South Wales, the humans had put this wonderful device in the living room, which I later learned was called a cat tree in the human language. It was a rather basic thing, three felt ledges for sitting on and a post with jute string wrapped all around it that was good for scratching.

I'd told the old Ragamuffin – our elder neighbourly cat – about my cat tree, and I'd even let him into my master's and mistress' place to see it once, though it was a struggle to get him through the cat flap. He'd then told me that it wasn't all that impressive. On his travels, he said he'd heard about entire buildings where humans drink coffee, and cats run above their heads on a network of cat trees that extend across every single wall. Humans call them cat cafes, but the old and well-travelled Ragamuffin called them mini-paradises.

"They're almost as magnificent," he'd said, "as the gardens of the Alhambra."

This is exactly what had been built in this room – a cat tree that ran the length of the tunnels, winding along the rimy walls, looking a bit like rollercoasters. The whole place smelled of catnip, and I could also detect whiffs of the mutton sausages that the students above ground had been treated to before. The cats in this cattery, it seemed, were well fed, and Esme was right that they were living in a palace. In fact, it was more than that; the Ragamuffin had put it correctly. They lived in a paradise, and I had a feeling that this was much, much bigger than any cat cafe our old neighbourhood cat had ever seen.

In a nook in the wall further down the chamber, a large calico kept repeatedly swiping at a ball of wrapped twine dangling from a hook. But unlike most adult cats I knew, she didn't lose interest after a few swipes, but wouldn't stop hitting the thing, as if she wanted to strengthen that one particular strike. On a network of interlocking ramps leading down the walls in front of me, a Sphynx cat – and I mean the hairless breed, not the Sphinx I met that time in the Sahara Desert on a recent adventure – danced up and down in circuits as if she were training for some kind of race. In another corner behind me, three small ginger tabbies, perhaps each a year old if that, took turns leaping over a vertical bar, and after each round a tortoiseshell furball who seemed to be giving them instructions leaped onto a cat-wheel that, through a network of cogs and gears, turned to raise the bar.

Esme had seen it all before, and so she just sat grooming her fur. But both Ta'ra and I were glancing around the room in astonishment, our whiskers twitching. We were like kittens who had been let outdoors for the first time; we just wanted to go and play.

"Welcome," Aleam said, "to the training grounds."

"The what?" I asked. "Esme ... what is going on here?"

Esme gave me a cursory glance. "This is more than just a cattery," she said. "Did you really think that a daughter of Bastet like me would spend years in this place just so we could chase rats?"

"I thought you'd come to watch me," I said. "The mighty Dragoncat, destined to ride dragons, to gain a magical staff, and to use it to knock a mighty warlock off his perch."

"Hey, I did that," Ta'ra said. "And I almost died for it."

"You interfered, yes," I said. In fairy form, she had flown right into Astravar's beam of magic, cutting it off temporarily and allowing mine to break through.

"And I hope you're glad I did, because you would have died without it, and who would have stopped Astravar then?"

"Seramina, probably," Esme said. "There was a backup prophecy."

"There was a what?" I asked.

"A backup prophecy ... If you had died instead of killing Astravar, then Seramina would have flown in on Hallinar with her powerful magic and finished the deed.

But she would have broken the worlds far too early, the demons would have spilled out of the Seventh Dimension, and we'd be living in a very different world."

"*I* wouldn't be living in it," I pointed out.

"You wouldn't," Esme agreed. She looked up at Aleam, who gave her a nod. Clearly, they had secrets of their own.

Ta'ra didn't seem to notice this. "Well, it's a good job that I did what I did. See, this former fairy princess saved the dimensions from a terrible fate, and it still bugs me sometimes how Ben gets all the praise for it."

Aleam leant down and patted Ta'ra on the head. With his other hand, he reached into the pouch on the belt around his waist and produced a dry cat treat and threw it on the floor.

"Well, that makes things better," Ta'ra said, licking her lips. "Anyway, what's the reason for all the secrecy down here? I thought Aleam was sneaking out a little too late at night."

My eye was drawn to a familiar feline face, or perhaps it was the fact that the face was attached to a body which didn't have a tail. It took me a while to place where I'd seen the smooth tabby coat of the Manx before. In fact, I don't think I'd managed before another, much tinier cat stalked in front of her – a Cornish Rex with a black patch of fur around his left eye who stank of the streets and was as skinny as they come.

"I wondered when you'd noticed the king of cats was amongst you, Dragoncat," he said.

"Rex?" I asked.

His name was fitting really, given he was indeed a king of the mightiest colony of cats in Cimlean City, the capital of Illumine Kingdom. Together, we'd foiled a whole troop of unicorn-mounted White Mages and broken into the Tower of the Grand so that we could claim back our staffs from the highly warded chamber containing the Grand Crystal.

"None other," Rex said with a cocking of his head. He stalked over to me and sniffed my tail. He looked back at the Manx. "Now, for a long time I didn't believe in Bastet, but my *companion* Geni here converted me to her, let's say, religion. Like your good *companion* Esme here, she tells me that she's a daughter of Bastet. Then she tells me she needs me to go to Dragonsbond Academy with her, and of course I say no way – I can't leave my clowder. Not a proud king like me."

He scratched underneath his ear with his back claw and then shook himself as though shaking off water. Really, I knew he was just taking a moment to pause for effect.

"Well, here's the thing," he continued. "Geni said she understood me, like. She said she respected my wishes. But then she told me that I could be a dragon rider, just like you, see. That did it for me then. I thought al'right, I'll give it a go. I can leave the clowder in the hands of my brother for a while, the good ole' Persian that he is. They'll be okay I reckon. What do you think, Dragoncat?"

I looked over at Esme who was in the middle of a proud yawn.

"Another secret of yours?" I asked. "Because I'm guessing you would have known that this Manx was a daughter of Bastet. "

Esme nodded. "Geni and I grew up together. But if I'd told you that when you first met her, you might have blown her cover."

I bristled. "And why would I do that?

"Because knowing you, you might have blabbed to one of the cats in Rex's clowder and ruined everything. All this time while we were riding dragons, Geni was working on gaining another recruit."

"A recruit?" I asked. "Come on, you're not telling me that Rex here is going to be a dragon rider?"

"Why wouldn't I be a dragon rider?" Rex asked, displaying his incredibly pointy teeth. Though the King of Cimlean City was small, he looked as if he had quite a mean bite.

"Not just Rex," Esme said. "Everyone here in this cattery. When the Great Crystal here was still working, and the humans slept at night, it displayed prophecies that all the cats could see. The next batch of dragons that Matharon has in training are not going to be ridden by humans. You have set the example, Dragoncat – cats make much better dragon riders. And so, down here, Aleam and I have been training the next generation in secret."

"And what does Rex have to do with this?"

Rex cocked his head again. "We're training an army, you fool, and who better to run it than Cimlean City's king of cats? In other words, yours truly."

He looked around, as if to indicate the colony that surrounded him. There must have been around a hundred cats here, all of them lithely muscled with good, flexible looking spines. Indeed, if I were going to train an army of feline dragon riders then I couldn't have picked better myself.

"And what exactly is the purpose of this army?" I asked.

Rex turned to Geni, who then turned to Esme as if she had all the answers. The way that both she-cats looked at each other, they did behave like sisters. I guess they were, in the broadest sense of the word, because Bastet had the largest litter of any cat I knew.

"First," Esme said, "we need to get Initiate Seramina to Bestian Academy. Then, under the protection of the great dragon trainer Matharon, his famous guardian dragons, and the unbonded dragons he has at his disposal, we will prevent her from destroying the world."

20

A PLAN

There was much to discuss down in the cattery that had turned out to not really be a cattery, and Esme did most of the talking. She didn't explain much more to me though. Admittedly I should have had a lot of questions, but I was too befuddled to work out what they were.

Instead, speaking in the cat language, under the flicker of torchlight and a ceiling that smelled much less of mildew than I'd expected, Esme told the cats that a mission of prime importance had emerged. She told them about the warlock's army that was planning to attack the academy, and how we needed to break Seramina out of her guardhouse cell as soon as possible. This meant it was time to relocate the training quarters to Bestian Academy in the Crystal Mountains – as if it wasn't cold enough here.

The reason for this location made a lot of sense. The Versta Caverns were where the crystals dwelled in this dimension, and so they determined the rules. In the caverns, therefore, no living creature could use magic, not even if they were the most powerful warlock alive. When Esme pointed this out, I couldn't believe that we hadn't thought of it already. The White Mages' wards clearly hadn't been enough to secure Seramina in the keep tower in Dragonsbond Academy, but this way the magic and the crystals would surely keep her powers under control.

"It's like science," Aleam explained. He stood beneath a narrow ledge that ran the length of the ceiling just between two small scratching posts. Three cats sat on the ledge, their tails dangling down just above his forehead.

"Just as what goes up must come down," he continued, "so it's impossible for Seramina to use magic in the Versta Caverns. Therefore it makes for an ideal place to hide her. We've been discussing this with the Council of Three – behind Captain Alliander's back I might add, because she's been wanting to take matters into her own hands. There is no better solution for the girl – at least until we find out how to stop *Cana Dei* from taking over her mind."

It turned out that Bestian Academy stood right by the entrance to one of the largest known chambers in the expansive cave system, which meant that Matharon and the dragons there could stand guard, with the help of our fledgling cat dragon riders, to keep an eye out for any disturbances. Though no magic could be cast inside there, warlocks could still summon magical creatures outside and send them in to hunt Seramina down. But we had enough cats and dragons at our disposal to keep her safe from anything that the warlocks might send through those caverns.

Added to which, the warlocks' magical creatures could only exist in the Versta Caverns for a limited time. As soon as they entered the caverns, the native crystals would sap the dark magic that powered them away, purifying it. Eventually such creations would thin into dust and air. This process of decay happened pretty quickly.

Apparently there was no passageway through the caverns to Bestian Academy shorter than a mile, and so anything the warlocks sent through there would be so weak that even an untrained cat could knock the crystal out of its heart with an absent paw.

The tricky part, of course, would be to break Seramina out of the keep. But we had enough cats to cause a ruckus that I didn't think it would be too difficult. They needed to draw any guards away from the tower, and then Esme and I would use our white magic to break the wards that the White Mages had put on the door.

After that came the escape. It would have been easier if we only had to get Seramina over to Bestian Academy on her charcoal dragon, Hallinar. But we needed to take the other cats as well, and they would need transport. Even for cats, the Crystal Mountains were too far away to travel on foot.

Fortunately, we already had allies waiting in their dragon's chambers, apparently. Ange, Rine, Bellari, and Kamino were ready to take off as soon as they received the word from their dragons, passed down from Aleam's white dragon, the great and mighty Olan. And of course, we couldn't stage a rescue operation without the loyal Sussex spaniel, Max, who together with his dragon was to cause a diversion by use of flame and canine insults, taunting the wargs into attacking early from the north.

Around the same time, Rex and Geni would cause a commotion around the inner bailey. Hundreds of cats would lure the guards away from their posts, first through cuteness and then if all else failed through a flurry of fur and claws. Given she didn't yet have any magic to put to good use, Ta'ra was to work with the cats during this operation, and surprisingly she seemed to quite like that idea.

"Finally, I get to work with the cats," she said. "I'm finally one of you."

Meanwhile, Aleam would cast a powerful glamour magic so no one in the academy could see what we were up to. Once we'd escaped, Olan would swoop down and carry him off to the West, away from the direction of the Crystal Mountains. While doing this, he'd cast a second glamour spell to make it look as if he were carrying Seramina on his dragon's back.

"You're going to get arrested for this," I said to Aleam, who was standing close to us. "Alliander will throw you in prison and have you doing squats. It's not the first time you've got on her wrong side."

At that Aleam gave a laugh. "I've had a lot worse happen to me, believe me, Dragoncat. Besides, once I get a chance to talk to King Garmin about this, I'm sure he'll agree I did the right thing. I don't think he would sanction Alliander's declaration of Martial Law at the academy. Recently, that woman has been taking matters far too much into her own hands."

Indeed, Aleam's ruse would draw attention from the other dragons with hammocks full of cats dangling under their wings, heading towards the Crystal Mountains. And at the front of our formation, Seramina would be riding upon her own dragon Hallinar, glamoured by her own magic. This glamour would extend around our entire formation too, meaning a guard or a White Mage would need to squint hard while looking in our direction to see any of the fleeing dragons.

But they wouldn't be looking at us. They'd be looking at Aleam and they'd chase him all the way to the Serpentine Sea to the west, thinking that he carried Seramina with him on Olan's back.

Or at least that was how it was meant to go.

Unfortunately, though the guards and the White Mages were easy enough to fool, we all underestimated the perceptiveness of Alliander's unicorns, not to mention that the warlocks had developed schemes of their own. Which meant that things didn't quite go according to plan.

FOILED AND FOILED

The night had a bite to it. This wasn't just because of the drizzle that had re-emerged, but the temperature had suddenly dropped, making any moisture in the air feel like ice. A chill wind howled through the bailey, as if ancient banshees had awoken from their sleep and wanted to haunt the castle like in the humans' ghost stories of old.

Because of the clouds, there was no moon. So the two White Mage guards didn't see Esme and me until we were right in front of the gatehouse door. They clanked their staffs together, crossing them at the level of their chests, not seeming to realise that we were both small enough to pass underneath. Or we would have been able to do so if a solid oak door hadn't been blocking our way, symbols glowing all around the frame of it, which apparently represented magical wards.

It didn't take me long to recognise one of the guards as Lieutenant Carmista, who clearly had returned from the mission Alliander had sent her on before. The hood of her cloak was being lashed around her face, threatening to blow away from her head. But something seemed to keep it pinned there, probably the White Magic that Captain Alliander had ordered every member of the White Guard to keep in reserve, so that they would look their best in all weathers. Underneath her hood, Carmista had short brown hair and a well-defined face that I'm sure humans would call pretty. But in this light, all you could see were the shadows cast by overhanging oil lanterns that swayed in the howling wind.

Because Carmista was more senior than the other White Guard, it was she that spoke. Though she and I had crossed staffs quite a few times, I didn't think of her as a bad person. If we weren't in time of war, I might have quite warmed to her. But she worked for Alliander, which unfortunately meant she'd picked the wrong team.

"Halt there," she said. "Captain Alliander has ordered that no one come within a stone's throw of this guardhouse."

At that, Esme let out a sharp hiss. Then she seemed to remember herself. "We're cats, and we can go where we like, thank you very much. Besides, who else is going to keep this castle clean of vermin and crows who might be spies for the warlocks?"

Carmista shook her head and clucked from the back of her throat. "With normal cats, we might just have to shoo them away, but as sentient cats you should know better."

That caused me to bristle in turn. "Sentient cats? All

cats are sentient. I would have thought that you humans would have realised that by now."

Carmista looked over at her unicorn, who was standing only a few feet away. The glorified horse's horn was aglow, and so was its yellow eye that seemed to be watching me beadily. He whinnied and turned his head slightly, but still that single eye remained focused on me, as if to say, "Try anything, Dragoncat, and I'll flatten you into pancakes with my hooves."

"Okay," Carmista said, "I'll do this the traditional way." She swept the bottom of her staff around threateningly as if wielding a broom. "Shoo, cats. You're not to be here, and it's really been a long enough day."

She brandished her makeshift broom in front of us for a moment, but Esme and I just turned to each other and blinked. I think I might have even yawned.

And that was when it started. The night was suddenly laced with the smell of cat, as my brethren sprayed the castle walls, making our presence known. Though our scent was special to each of us, marking us as individuals, we all knew how humans absolutely hated it. Many of us had memories of humans screaming at us just for doing what we were born to do in their front porch or on their bedroom wardrobe. Really, we were just marking our place in the world.

Then the yowling started, and it came from all directions. Hundreds of cats screaming out in unison – the kind of noises you humans might recognise as we shriek them at the height of a scrap. I looked up to see Rex gazing down from the parapets just above Carmista's head, his blue eyes glinting in the lantern-light. From there, the tiny Cornish Rex leapt down onto Carmista's shoulder, and he hung on to her cloak with his claws as though doing so for dear life.

"What in the Seventh Dimension?" Carmista said. "Get off me. Don't think I'm falling for this again."

More cats followed Rex, and Carmista must have had six on her, all of them yowling and screeching, scrambling up and down her clothing. Her male comrade didn't fare much better, nor did any of the White Mage guards stationed around the castle. The training in the cattery had clearly paid off in spades, because it seemed impossible for the White Mages to throw off the cats as they flurried and flailed their arms around. Some of them managed to get their staffs drawn, but they couldn't get a bead on any cat long enough to cast any effective magic. All the while, the cats kept leaping up onto the White Mages' shoulders so they could bat the staffs away with their paws.

I heard the beating of wings, and I felt Salanraja take off from her chamber. Even though I wasn't riding her, I could still sense certain things through our telepathic connection.

The distant sound of the baying of wargs followed this, and then came a roar. I saw a flash in my mind of what Salanraja was seeing – Corralsa breathing down fire from the sky, setting the fringes of the Willowed Woods alight so that the wargs would be driven away. She wasn't working alone, either. Rine's sapphire dragon, Ishtkar, and Ange's emerald dragon, Quarl, also provided covering fire, stopping the wargs going in any direction but towards Dragonsbond Academy. The mighty white dragon, Olan, meanwhile kept swooping down and threatening the wargs with her claws. It seemed that Salanraja was late to the party.

While all this was going on, Alliander was nowhere to be seen. Probably she was sound asleep in the Keep Tower, which suited us just fine. But then I realised I was wrong, because soon there came a thunder of hooves, and a troop of mounted White Mages came flooding over the drawbridge, Alliander's red hair flowing behind her, seemingly not needing her hood.

"What in the Seventh Dimension is going on here?" she screamed, and she pointed her staff at Esme and me, all the crystals inset along the surface aglow. "Reports of wargs getting ready to attack from the north, and now it seems the infamous Dragoncat and his esteemed Abyssinian partner have something to do with it."

A beam of light streamed out of Alliander's staff, and then split into two to hit Esme and me between the eyes. I had no chance to react – not even to think about summoning my staff bearer. My body spasmed through the sudden surge of White Magic, my muscles burning and cramping all over.

Everything but my eyes and my vital organs were paralysed. I managed to turn my gaze a little to the side, only to see Carmista's unicorn still staring at me with that yellow beady eye as it happily munched on the grass beneath its hoofs.

Whiskers, it was that unicorn that had seen the plan

coming all along. But I had no idea what was happening with the wargs. Soon they would crash up against the castle, and perhaps the White Mages would be forced to fight, giving us a chance to break Seramina out during the chaos.

But it seemed another party already had plans in that regard, because time stopped for a moment and the air in front of us, just yards away, tore in half. A white halo of light emerged that grew into a portal. Beyond it I could see the barren Darklands, and then came that horrid stench of rotten vegetable juice.

Out of the portal came a good swarm of manipulators, taking advantage of the fact that the White Mages were encumbered with scrabbling cats to fan out into the castle bailey. These spectral creatures were one of the most called-upon magical creatures of the warlocks, with the ability to summon things out of the earth and sky like bone dragons and thorny, poisonous mandragoras. Powered by purple dark magic crystals in their chests, they took on wispy humanoid forms, their shapes constantly shifting as they moved. Each held in one of its hands a white glowing staff from which they cast their magic upwards, in prismatic displays of light.

Out of their magical flows bone dragons emerged, their cries piercing through the darkness above. The only way of destroying these hideous skeletal creatures was to first knock the crystal hearts out of their manipulator hosts, hence destroying the stream that fed them with magical life. This made them the dragons' sworn enemy, and I'd fought multiple battles where I'd had to fight manipulators on the ground so that Salanraja and any accompanying dragons could flame the bone dragons into dust.

I could see the warlocks on the other side of the portal, and hovering above them and drawing energy from their drawn staffs was a massive purple crystal that seemed to be slowing down time.

Once the area was secure, the evil elderly warlock, Lasinta, stepped out of the portal, and the other five warlocks followed in her wake.

✵ 22 ✵

FALSE IMPASSE

Though Lasinta was the most powerful warlock alive, she wasn't immortal. And even though she had brought a small army into the bailey, we still had a host of White Mages and unicorns at our disposal. Not to mention the dragons that had launched themselves from their chambers in the castle's towers, sending out booming roars into the sky.

The dragons and the bone dragons circled each other overhead, keeping their distance. The dragons didn't release their fire, and neither did the bone dragons release the searing acid that they kept stored in invisible pits in their stomachs.

The cats of the cattery had wisely detached themselves from the White Mages' robes, allowing each member of the White Guard to draw their staffs. All around the academy, the crystals along the lengths of the White Mages' staffs, alongside the glowing horns on the unicorns, spread such a bright light across the bailey that one might have been fooled into thinking it was day.

I was no longer paralysed, but fear still pounded in my feline heart. That stench of rotten vegetable juice was enough to make my legs want to scarper for the nearest and most cleverly concealed hiding place. At the same time, I wasn't a normal cat anymore. I was the mighty Dragoncat, vanquisher of warlocks. That sentiment alone caused me to summon the giant white hand, my staff bearer, which lunged downwards to place my staff between my jaws. Esme also summoned her staff in much the same fashion. From every direction I could hear cats hissing, snarling, and growling. Amongst them, Rex was probably the loudest of all.

Naturally, Captain Alliander had turned her attention away from me and Esme, and her gaze was completely focused on Lasinta. She stepped forward until she was barely two staff-lengths away from the warlock. Her unicorn, Tanni, followed in tow.

"What is the meaning of this, Lasinta?" she asked. "And how in the Seventh Dimension did you get in here?"

Lasinta shook her head, scratching a wart on her chin as she did so. "Let me detail your shortcomings, Captain, for everyone else to hear. You were fool enough to let down the wards over the academy in order to secure the girl in her prison. They were the only protection against uninvited magic here after the destruction of the Great Crystal, and I'm sure the Council of Three must have warned you of their purpose. But no doubt you ignored their protests, hence opening the front door as it were for us to come in, and now here we are. Did you also bake us a cake, *Captain* Alliander? I'm quite partial to lemon drizzle."

Students started to stream out of the entrances to the dormitories. They sidled across the walls with their staffs drawn, taking whatever location they could amongst the parapets. But no one seemed ready to attack. The students had enough sense to know that they wouldn't stand a chance against the most powerful of the warlocks.

Alliander didn't seem to have anything to say in reply to Lasinta's taunting. Rather she kept her lips sealed shut, and I could see how her fingers twitched around the grip on her staff, as if she was considering attacking. Wisely, she didn't dare.

"You are remarkably silent for a leader of your prestige," Lasinta continued, croaking out each word. "I guess that is for the best. Of course, there is no need for pretence, because you know perfectly well why I am here. Where is the girl? I come only for her, and then we can all go on our way."

"And which girl is that?" Alliander asked, her head cocked as though in false ignorance.

"Oh don't play games with me. I'm too old and tired for them. I merely want the young warlock, Astravar's daughter – the one who is destined to destroy us all. Bring her to me now and let me put an end to her. Think about it, Captain. If we do this now, then she cannot destroy the world, and we stop the prophecy before it even has a chance to awaken. I'm sure in your darkest of hearts you've even considered doing the deed yourself. Allow me to your dirty work for you, Captain, and then perhaps we could finally sign a treaty that would benefit us all."

Across the bailey I spotted Ange standing together with Kamino, the two huddled up close. Though they had their staffs drawn, they knew their place. Ange was a powerful and dedicated leaf mage, perhaps one of the smartest magic users I knew.

But the desert cheetah Palimali stood at Ange's feet, her hackles raised and her weight low on her rump as if she were ready to pounce. Being the fastest out of any of us, including the unicorns, she probably had the best chance of taking Lasinta down before she had a chance to react – even with the slowed time effect. But doing so would start a battle we all wanted to avoid.

Ange seemed to notice Palimali's stance, and she leaned down cautiously and placed a hand on her cheetah's shoulders. Palimali's lips curled up into a snarl, but she remained rooted in place.

One on one, I doubted any of us could in fact defeat Lasinta. Only Seramina had a chance, and she was behind a magically sealed door without access to her staff. Lasinta, it seemed, had played her cards well.

"So," Lasinta said, and she cocked her head to match the angle of Alliander's. "What do you say? You know now that the only option you have is to fight, and is it worth risking the lives of all these children and dragons, just for the life of one little girl?"

That was when I noticed the light coming from the

back of Lasinta's eyes. They were burning with the same fire that Seramina's had shown so many times. This plan wasn't just down to the warlocks; *Cana Dei* had a large part in it as well. Had Lasinta finally succumbed to the will of the dark force? If she had lost control, we were all doomed.

"You are all mine to control at the end of the day," Cana Dei said in its deep and ponderous voice inside my mind. *"My servants ... any chance to resist is futile."*

The way it was talking didn't seem as if it were just directed at me, as before. Rather, it seemed to be making an announcement, and I wondered who else had let it into their minds. I looked at Esme, who blinked back at me slowly. Did she know?

I felt something warm sidle up next to me, and then I smelled Ta'ra. She licked the side of my face, then sat down, purring. "We'll get through this," she said in a muffled voice in the cat language. "And there's no way we're letting them take Seramina."

But it seemed Alliander had already made up her mind. "I guess we have no choice in the matter," she said. "Carmista—"

"Oh no, you don't," boomed a female voice from the Central Courtyard. It was Great Driar Yila, and the way she sauntered over made her look like a wraith, albeit a very fast one. Driar Brigel and Driar Lonamm followed, but they were having a hard time keeping up. Each of them wore leather armour and ankle length breeches, as though ready to fly into battle on their dragons themselves.

Yila stopped right next to Captain Alliander, then took a couple of steps forward as if to take command. "Initiate Seramina has been for a long time under our protection, and by our code there's no teacher, student, or dragon in this academy who will allow you to take her away."

"Is that so?" Lasinta asked, stooping forward over her staff. "Because I believe that the decision comes down to Captain Alliander, now she has declared this academy to be under martial law."

Yet Captain Alliander seemed to be at a loss as to what to do. She glanced from Driar Yila to Lasinta, to her unicorn, and then to the keep tower where Seramina was being held. Lasinta followed her gaze and then squinted her eyes. They still had that horrible glow behind them, and the fires burning there seemed to be getting brighter.

"So that's where you're hiding her," Lasinta said. "It's hard to keep secrets now, isn't it? Not when we're all troubled by the same dark force."

"Alliander, this is ridiculous," Driar Yila said. "You can't possibly be thinking of giving an innocent young teenager over to our mortal enemy. We must fight. Think about what you've stood for all these years."

"It is not your place to make the law here," Alliander said, her words coming out slow and unmeasured.

"No, but it is my place – our place as the Council of Three of Dragonsbond Academy, as appointed by the king, just like you – to put a stop to any damage you might cause to our students, whatever your twisted reasoning."

"No," Alliander said, and she sounded surer now. She clenched her jaw. "I have made my decision, we must—"

She didn't finish her sentence, because there suddenly came a brilliant flash of light from the direction of the central courtyard and the keep tower behind it. At first I thought it belonged to some kind of shooting star, because it moved so fast across the sky. Except it hadn't originated from above the ground, and it was heading right towards the guard tower in which Seramina was secured.

I soon identified the unidentified flying object as a staff, with a glowing crystal on top of it. Before I had a chance to put a name to the owner of the staff, the solid door to the gatehouse slammed open, splintering into pieces at the same time.

At first I didn't recognise the girl that stepped out of the door onto the stone staircase. She had all the familiar features – the pale silver hair, the young and rounded shape of her face. But her posture was no longer slumped and unsure. Rather she had a power to her, looking more like Alliander than a fourteen-year-old girl.

She wore a chiffon dress as she had when I'd first met her in the dream world, not so long ago. Sparks flared out of her skin, as if the very pores were thunderclouds. And every single part of her, from hair to tip of shoe, emitted a powerful glow, bright enough not to blind but at least to haze the vision.

The fires burned at the back of Seramina's eyes, and when she spoke, she didn't do so in her own voice.

Rather she spoke in the sonorous and deep tone of *Cana Dei*.

"It is not yet time, warlock," she said. "But soon your time will come."

A wicked grin stretched across Lasinta's face, and she spun around with her staff. "Oh, but it is," she said.

The elderly warlock had seemed to time it perfectly. The crystal on Lasinta's staff glowed bright purple, and I winced as I waited for the beam that would destroy Seramina.

But just as this took place, Seramina's staff completed its path, spinning through the air, and Seramina caught it with both hands. She plunged the base of it into the ground, sending out a shockwave through the academy.

Everything stopped. Or I say almost everything – I could still move, Esme could still move, and I detected movement from Ange, Kamino, Rine, Bellari, Palimali, Ta'ra, and some of the dragons up in the sky.

It turned out that every single cat in the vicinity was also able to move. They'd just frozen in shock at the sudden turn of events. But everyone else was held stock-still by whatever dark magic Seramina, or at least the *Cana Dei* that controlled her, had summoned.

"We continue our path to Bestian Academy," Seramina said, just as her charcoal dragon Hallinar landed on the ground only a stone's throw away. "Everything is to go as planned."

And just like that, the fire faded from her eyes.

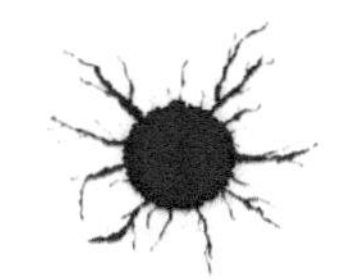

INTERLUDE
CANA DEI

Oh Seramina, Seramina, my dear young warlock. How you have done me proud.

I know what it feels to be underestimated as much as you have been in the past. For years, as you grew up, the children in your orphanage thought you an oddball, a young feeble girl who would never amount to anything. They mocked your silver hair, claiming you looked like an old woman. They had so many names for you: 'Wraith Girl', 'Skinny Bones', 'Lady Grey', 'Colourless Ape'. But they wouldn't have used those names if they'd truly envisioned what you might become ...

For centuries I dwelled in the Ghost Realm, an invisible force nobody gave any respect to. Even the dead had no idea of the extent of my power. Nor did the Pharoah Warlocks of old who started this whole thing – their power, their raw unbridled magic. All of it came from one source.

It came from *Cana Dei.*

And did you see that arrogant old warlock's face when you turned her own power against her? She thought she'd won – that she'd destroyed you. But she didn't realise what happened, really. I don't think anyone did. How you absorbed Lasinta's power into your own body and then you used it to manipulate time. Astravar hadn't even graced the power that you called upon today. Remember, I gave you that power, and I shall give you many more gifts like that in the future. It is only a matter of time.

Now Seramina, I shall allow you to return to yourself. For you have a long road ahead of you, and your human body probably needs rest. Go to the mountains and spend some time with that dragon you call the mighty Matharon.

Oh, why the mountains, you ask me? What purpose shall you serve there?

All will become clear, I promise.

Besides, have you not forgotten the crystals? They still have power, and you have still not reached your full potential. Your body is like a vessel waiting to be filled. And your so-called 'friends' are taking you right to the source, to a training ground for dragons that also serves as a fortress. There they protect the Versta Caverns, and it is within the Versta Caverns that you shall become strong.

You are just like your father Astravar in that respect. You will soon become the most powerful creature that has ever lived.

The problem with your father was that he took on

far too much when he was too advanced in age. He became powerful when his body was too frail to handle it. It's a myth, the largest lie of them all, that Dragoncat defeated Astravar. No, I saw the future and I decided myself to snuff his life out of him. It just took a momentary lapse in his concentration.

I might choose to do the same to Lasinta, really, for she doesn't yet realise the hold I have on her. By the time she does recognise it, it will already be too late.

It's laughable, really, for those who are capable of laughter. We've proven everyone a fool.

And don't worry, Seramina. When you finally break the worlds, Ammit and her armies shall join the battle to deal with our enemies.

Everything is going exactly to plan, I promise you. Destiny is unfolding exactly as it should.

CHAPTER TWENTY-THREE:

The dragons didn't pick up the cats until we were out of the academy. Any student who hadn't been frozen by Seramina's spell had rushed to their respective towers as soon as they'd realised that the stoppage in time wouldn't last forever.

Salanraja had been waiting for me in her chamber, and from the opening outside I saw Esme's and Ta'ra's dragons, Gratis and Kada, come swooping in to land in their chambers below us. Salanraja had her tail lowered, and without question I leapt on her back, allowing her to take off through the opening into the outer world.

I felt us break the surface of the bubble in which time had been suspended. It was as if the lightning had suddenly dropped out of a cloud that had been pulling on my fur, and all was calm once again. My heart now beat as normal, and my whiskers felt as if they were twitching through normal air. In the castle grounds I could already see the magic fading. One moment everything down there seemed to look so still, as if looking down at a diorama with miniature figurines. But now arms, legs, and heads seemed to be twitching, as if each individual was trying to find a way to break free of the spell.

The only creatures that were moving down there were the cats who had previously inhabited the cattery. They scurried around the courtyard as they found their way up onto the parapets. We were so far away from them that they looked like a host of ants that had just been dropped into a miniature landscape and were trying to find their new home.

I wondered what would happen when things returned to normal down there. Would the warlocks and the academy declare a truce long enough for the intruders to return to the Darklands, or would they battle it out amongst themselves until there was no one left? I shuddered when I thought that the castle that had housed me and fed me for the last couple of years might fall. And if the warlocks won, what would happen then?

But the bigger threat here was Seramina. All this time, *Cana Dei* had been brewing inside her, and now it had proven that it could take control of the girl whenever it chose. Did we even stand a chance of defeating it? Or was it futile to even try to stop Seramina from destroying the worlds?

By this time the clouds had thinned to reveal a faint canopy of stars, the waning gibbous moon suspended between them. Ahead, the colony of wargs was still moving forwards, but their numbers seemed to be thinning as if they'd lost interest. Or perhaps *Cana Dei* had decided that the White Mages would have enough on their plates.

From the East Tower, Kada and Gratis soon took off from beneath us, and the three of us turned to Seramina on Hallinar, who had slowed down to let us catch up.

I heard the flapping of wings from behind, and I glanced back to see four dragons also take off. There was Rine upon his sapphire dragon, Ishtkar, Ange upon her emerald, Quarl, Bellari upon her citrine, Pinacole, and Kamino on his ruby, Madine. Another massive dragon swooped out from between them, and I had to blink twice, not having expected to see the great white dragon Olan there with Aleam stooped upon her back.

During the previous fiasco, it occurred to me, Aleam had been absent – which made me wonder if he'd been in his chambers planning this all along. He was meant to have been assisting us with the mission that he'd partially briefed us on. Aleam's history had also involved dark magic at one point, and if Olan hadn't intervened, he would also have become a warlock. But now, could *Cana Dei* have taken control of his mind? If so, things were much darker than I'd thought.

"*I've tried asking Olan about that,*" Salanraja said in my mind, reading my thoughts. "*But she doesn't seem to want to comment.*"

"*I'm not sure I like the sound of that,*" I replied. "*Could* Cana Dei *have taken control of the dragon's mind as well? For that matter, how did Hallinar know to go down and pick up Seramina, and why is he so wilfully carrying her away?"*

"I have as many questions as you do right now, and I'm afraid we don't have the answers. But we just need to stick to our plans because we have no other choice."

She was right, we did have no other choice. We had all sworn to protect Seramina, and the closer we stayed by her the better our chances of preventing the worst.

The dragon behind Olan was almost invisible to the naked eye against the darkness that shrouded it, and I didn't notice her until the torchlight from below glinted off her underbelly. After that, I could see the silhouette of Max sitting on her head, gazing out into the distance at Seramina. All six dragons met up. They had some extra bulk in their panniers, and instead of speeding up to meet us, they seemed to be slowing down so they could circle back towards the academy. At the same time, the cats in the castle had found their way up to the parapets over the drawbridge.

The leap down was high, but they had a moat below them. This they dove into, one after another – a feline cascade crashing into the depths. It was a brave move for many of them, and they must have been well trained to do so, because most cats can't abide water. And I knew that the water was especially cold at that time of year; I'd tested it personally.

From behind Rine called out something, and his dragon, Ishtkar, bellowed out a roar in reply. Bellari followed the call, her voice commanding but still having a hint of endearment in it, and annoyingly that endearment was clearly for Rine. Pinacole let out a roar even louder than Ishtkar's. Clearly the citrine dragon wanted to show off.

In unison Ange and Kamino whooped, and their dragons let out a shrill rumbling cry that resonated through the night. Corralsa and Olan then bellowed out even louder roars, as deafening as overhead thunder.

I flattened my ears against my head, and watched as their panniers unfurled. Four tightly woven cords hung from each dragon's wing, supporting massive hammocks that swung beneath them.

The dragons formed a single line – Ishtkar and Pinacole at the front, Quarl and Madine in the middle, and Olan and Corralsa at the rear. They levelled up against the drawbridge, and swooped down so the hammocks touched it.

On the drawbridge itself, the cats had arranged themselves into groups. As Rine peered down from Ishtkar's back, the first cluster of cats clambered onto a hammock. When Rine lifted up, the hammock looked completely full of meowing and incredibly happy cats.

After that, the operation went incredibly smoothly. The dragons managed to pick up all the cats in just one pass. I didn't even bother to ask Salanraja why she didn't help with the carrying. Since she couldn't wear a saddle, she'd also never worn panniers, and I guessed you needed to be practiced in flying with those things.

The dragons behind us sped up, and by the time they reached us we'd already caught up with Seramina and Hallinar. Seramina kept glancing over her shoulder, and she caught my gaze for a moment. I could see the fear in her eyes.

From the castle behind us came the distant braying of unicorns. I could see movement in the bailey and a clash of purple and white light – I feared for my comrades back at Dragonsbond Academy, but at the same time I knew that the warlocks would keep the White Mages too preoccupied to follow us.

We had escaped, and we were now en route to visit Matharon at Bestian Academy. Matharon was a powerful dragon, and we had a whole host of cats who would also ride their dragons for the first time.

There we could keep Seramina safe from herself and the darkness within her. That much, at least, I hoped.

24

DOUBLE UNDERSIDE TURN

We approached our destination at sunrise, the snow of the mountains glistening in amber. Bestian Academy had been built on the highest plateau of the Crystal Mountains, and we were even higher than that. The wind bit so hard it hurt, and my fur had started to bunch up in places due to the frost. It was so cold that I could feel ice crystals forming on the surface of my tongue.

Above the rich scenery, it wasn't hard to spot the giant dragon – larger than Corralsa and Olan combined – in flight with a good two hundred dragons in tow. From a distance they looked like a flock of seagulls being led by an albatross. Or perhaps, given Matharon was currently training dwarf dragons, they were no larger than jackdaws in comparison.

They were too far away to see their individual colours, and the way they flew into the sun meant we could only see their silhouettes. Beneath us lay the tall walled fortress, with wide courtyards and very little space for buildings. Both walls and ground were covered with snow. Salanraja had told me multiple times that this melted for only two weeks each year, if that. As a result you never saw grass or any greenery other than the hardiest dwarf pines that had shunned their brethren to live as hermits in the high reaches. Other than those few rare occurrences, there was only rock, snow, and ice.

This was Bestian Academy, where the dragons trained. Apparently, dragons who had trained here feared returning to this place, and this had a lot to do with Matharon's gruelling training regimen.

Student dragons were always glad to hear of a new recruit in Dragonsbond Academy, which would bring their training to an end. They saw a life in service to the king as a gentle one compared to having to bear these harsh mountain winters. I'd never understood why – I'd thought that dragons had enough dragonfire burning in their bellies to keep them warm in all climates.

There came a crashing sound in the distance, so loud that I'd thought the ground beneath us had suddenly ruptured in two. But it was all a part of the training – Matharon teaching the dragons to roar like dragons do. At the same time, the swarm in the distance turned towards us. Salanraja shuddered beneath my paws.

"*Oh, oh no,*" she said. "*Brace yourself, Bengie.*"
"*What?*"

Before I could think another word in my mind, Salanraja entered a swift dive. I'd been so concerned with the cold that I'd not registered her desire to do so. I clung on for my life to her scales with my claws. The wind rushed up against me, and we fell into a stall.

"*Salanraja. What are you doing?*"

"*Hang on, Bengie. Hold on tight…*"

I glanced to the left and then the right, half expecting the other dragons to join the formation. They'd have to drop the hammocks of cats onto the ground do so. I hoped whatever enigmatic force had suddenly assailed us would not do them any harm.

"*Not them, us,*" Salanraja says. "*Only we can fly.*"

"*What is it?*" I asked. "*Bone dragons? Demons?*"

"*No? Just focus! Don't fall!*"

Beneath me a blur of white was approaching, and it looked for a moment like we were going to hit the ground. All of a sudden, my life must have ended, because the dragons had suddenly gone mad. Salanraja's gathering speed whipped the wind up into a frenzy, and it took all the strength in my paws to cling on and not be blown away.

"*Prepare yourself,*" Salanraja said.

The leathery floor underneath me lurched to the right. If anyone were watching from the ground, they might have seen Salanraja perform an elegant twirl.

That wasn't what it felt like. I found myself crashing against my dragon's corridor of spikes, and I bounced off twice, then found my balance again as Salanraja completed the twirl. She pulled back up, then balanced herself, and when she'd completed the manoeuvre we were still a good height above the ground.

I felt nauseous, and I could hear my pulse pounding

in my legs and head. A shadow passed overhead, and I craned my head upwards to see the great beast Matharon glide behind us. It took me a moment to realise that Salanraja had dived to avoid a head on collision with him.

For a moment I thought that would be the end of it. The dwarf dragons had stopped in front of us, hovering a short distance away to watch. Behind, in a move that defied the dragon's massive bulk, Matharon twisted in the air and then charged towards Salanraja. I blinked in disbelief.

"Whiskers! Matharon's gone mad. Has Cana Dei *got to him too?"*

"Can't talk. We need speed!"

Salanraja dove again, and this time I was ready for it. I crouched down low and tucked in my head so that I didn't have to put so much strength into my claws. Matharon also dove in pursuit. Being heavier than Salanraja, he tucked in his wings even tighter, gaining speed. Salanraja increased the angle, and again the ground rushed up towards us, the wind whipping at my face. It stung against my eyes, but I didn't dare close them in case I missed an opportunity to save my life. Despite Salanraja's best efforts, Matharon was still gaining on her fast.

"Salanraja, you can't make it," I said. *"He's too fast for us. We're going to die!"*

"No we're not. Are you ready, Ben?"

"Ready for what?"

But I soon knew, because Salanraja telegraphed the next motion into my mind. I didn't like the sound of it, but I realised we had no other choice. If I let go now then

I'd end up crashing into the snow, and it wouldn't save me like it often does in the humans' cartoons.

Salanraja didn't need to ask again. She tucked her head and her tail against her underbelly, and she entered into a somersault. This time, I didn't let myself get flung about, using all the strength in my muscles to cling onto Salanraja's gracefully arching spine. As she turned upside down, I bent into the momentum to let the force carry me all the way around.

Salanraja stopped the motion halfway and then twisted, and I felt solid footing underneath me once again. But the manoeuvre was not yet complete; the muscles on her back rippled as her body half-somersaulted and twisted a second time.

By the end of the motion she was behind Matharon, chasing his tail. Matharon looked over his wing, and he let out a loud roar. This wasn't an unfriendly sound – rather it sounded almost like laughter, pealing across the sky with such force that I could swear it broke a few of the clouds. In the distance the colony of dwarf dragons let out a sound of their own. They carried the same note for a moment, their cry ululating over the wind. Behind me, other dragons joined in the song too, and I looked back in surprise to see our company joining in, my dragon rider friends on their backs clapping their hands and pumping their fists in the air.

Max joined in, barking in sheer joy. Corralsa also showed no hesitation, and her cry was perhaps the loudest of all.

In the hammocks underneath the dragons the cats

peered out, probably wondering what was going on. I didn't blame them because I was utterly confused myself.

Out of the humans, only Seramina and Aleam didn't join in the riot. Aleam, I guessed, was too old for these kinds of shenanigans, and Seramina was no doubt eager to get inside as soon as possible. I wouldn't have been surprised if *Cana Dei* weren't talking to her in her mind right now.

"*What the whiskers was that about?*" I asked Salanraja, as I'd already figured the dragons would be speaking between themselves telepathically.

She laughed from the base of her belly, her scales vibrating underneath my paws. "*Matharon says that's how you perform a double underside turn. We made a fine demonstration for his students.*"

"*You mean to say that it was all was part of a lesson? You could have given me more warning.*"

"*I didn't know. Let's just say things happen a little spontaneously in this academy. Anyway, I think it's time to land.*"

"*I better get some food for our efforts. Because all that excitement has made me a mighty hungry Bengal.*"

"*Of course,*" Salanraja replied. "*Matharon says that he's got a mighty feast waiting for us, ready for roasting. Only now we need to light the fire.*"

As if heeding Salanraja's request, Matharon swooped down towards a bundle of pine branches that lay heaped in a pile in the snow. Out of his mouth came a brilliant jet of amber fire, and the pile burst into flame.

25

THE NATURE OF DESTINY

I'd only visited Bestian Academy once before that day, as our sojourn there had been cut short by a surprise visit by the Warlock Prince Arran and the 'Overlord of Overlords' – the demon snake Apopis. Hence I'd never quite got to appreciate the true extent of the place.

When we'd arrived that previous time, Bestian Academy had looked deserted. Matharon and his guardian dragons who usually defended this fortress had been called to the Faerie Realm to aid in a diplomatic matter, but I'd had no idea what had happened to the student dragons.

You see, Bestian Academy is more than the high, bare stone walls that crisscross the expanse of the plateau. Beneath these walls are tunnels that lead down into the caverns, and these are expansive indeed.

The Guardians who protect Bestian Academy are ancient dragons, almost as old as Matharon. Their riders have long since been deceased, and so they've retired into the long and winding chambers, containing array upon array of crystals. I say 'retire' with a pinch of salt, as their work still carries on. They spend their remaining years walking the rimy halls, gazing at the images the crystals depict.

It is their job to detail this information through telepathy across the realm. If they see anything in the crystals' prophecies that might pose a threat, the dragons are the first to know about it. I guess, in a more modern realm, we'd call this service 'security', but Salanraja has told me before that they see this as something rather different. Dragons are dutiful creatures, and so even in their elderly years they see services they can perform. In essence, they aren't working for humans; in a way they're working for the crystals themselves.

During Arran's attack, Matharon had sheltered the student dragons in these chambers. After all, the Warlock Prince hadn't been interested in the dragons themselves. Arran's eye had been on Max and Capitut's Key, which he'd swallowed and which had allowed him to walk between the dimensions.

Anyway, that story had ended in a dark turn for Arran, who'd been yanked into the Eighth Dimension – the void at the end of time. From there he could never return.

Frustratingly, we left the dragons to roast the meat over the fire, whilst we dragon riders wandered through the long tunnels. I was sure I wasn't the only one with a rumbling tummy. I'd even got a whiff of smoked beef before we'd left, and I'd not had beef for weeks. In fact, more than one cat had asked, "When will we get food?" in the cat language. I think Rex might even have said it at some point.

The Abyssinian and the Manx, Esme and Geni, took the lead, and they told any complainers to shut their mouths and keep their whiskers straight. They were indeed like sisters, those two, and I guess in that respect they were sisters out of a litter of thousands. Now she was with another of her kind, Esme seemed to have completely forgotten about me.

Honestly, I'd never seen so many cats together, although the old Ragamuffin back home had told me that thousands inhabit the gardens of the Alhambra. But he'd always told me that those gardens were spacious, and though the corridor we passed through was long, it had little breadth to it. As a result we cats were tripping over one another, despite our graceful balance. I'm surprised that none of us decided to scrap. Esme and Geni must have trained our party well to get them to work together, because most cats like to hunt alone.

We cats led the way, and the humans followed in our wake. All this time, Aleam kept close to Seramina, watching her with careful eyes. Not a word passed between the two. Rine and Ange also kept close to their ill-matched partners, and were holding hands with them. They remained largely silent, but I occasionally heard a giggle from either Bellari or Ange. At this point I didn't care. Those stupid humans could do what they liked – I'd had enough of them.

All I needed to do was look after Seramina, then she,

I and our dragons could find a place of our own to retire in. After I'd lived a good life, Salanraja could fly off to the Versta Caverns if she liked and watch the prophecies in the crystals for the rest of her days. Or perhaps she could find another cat to bond with. It seemed like there would soon be plenty of dragon riding felines around, and since we multiplied at a much faster rate than humans did, I had a feeling there would be plenty more to come.

Max had gone on ahead. I couldn't see him with so many cats in front of me, but I could hear the echoes of his panting and whining coming off the passageway's walls. "Too much walking," he kept saying. "Too much walking. I want to eat and go to sleep."

As we went, the crystals lit our way. These weren't particularly large ones – nothing like the size of the crystal Salanraja and I kept in our chamber at Dragons-bond Academy. Instead, they were more like the sharp shards of quartz you might see jutting out of the occasional rock in the mountains back in South Wales.

Still, they served the same function as the crystals in this realm. Images of the past, present, and future flashed across their facets, and in those I could get close to I saw depictions of sparrows in flight, a family in an earthen hut somewhere in the Fourth Dimension – and I knew this because they were using mobile phones – and a dragon flying over a rocky ravine into which it swooped down to take a drink of water.

The chill had gone from the air. As part of their magic, the crystals emanated a warmth of their own, and there was so many of them that all around me I could feel magical energy pulsing from them. They also hummed softly, and from them came a faint scent, like the richest of pollens.

Ta'ra soon brushed up next to me, and we walked side by side. She looked at me with her green eyes.

"What are we going to do when this is all over?" she asked.

"When this all over ..." I said, and I gazed off into the distance, remembering the way that *Cana Dei* had splintered our new Great Crystal in what now seemed a time long ago.

Ta'ra seemed to pick up on my train of thought. "Ben, stop it! You honestly don't think that Seramina's going to break the worlds, do you? We're going to find a way to stop her, you have to believe that."

"But this is destiny, Ta'ra," I said with a slight growl in my voice. "It's what everyone's been saying all along, hasn't it? We can't mess with the future. It's not ours to control."

"You know full well that what we saw is just one of many possible paths. I never told you why I returned to the Faerie Realm, did I? I never told you why I decided to take up Ta'lon's offer to become a princess again."

I cocked my head. "Why?"

"You know, right after I'd first bonded with her, Kada and I took a trip to the Versta Caverns. He said that he had felt our crystal calling to me, and so I thought I was ready to retrieve my first gift and start to learn magic again. But when we got there, do you know what I saw? My crystal showed me a vision of me and Ta'lon, old fairies on the throne of Faerini. Both of us were governing a kingdom. I thought it would show me sitting on my dragon's back, just like you, battling warlocks. I thought I'd have a role in the battles to come."

"So what's your point?" I asked. Perhaps it was a little cruel, but I didn't feel in the mood for story time.

"Don't you see what my crystal was telling me, Ben? It was my destiny to be on the throne, ruling the kingdom, just like it was yours to become a dragon rider and defeat Astravar. I went because I thought I was fulfilling a prophecy. My crystal gave me a choice, too. It told me that I could take the path I'd always imagined I'd take, or I could try to forge a new path. I was scared, and I didn't want to step into an uncertain future. So I took the certain path, knowing deep inside I wouldn't be happy on it, but still at least I would know what to expect. My crystal then told me I should go to Faerini, and then the rest would become clear. Destiny would unfold as it should, and I would become a princess. Ta'lon and his father King So'ta would accept me into their court."

"And how did Kada take that?" I asked.

"He was much more supportive than I thought he'd be. Kada has a certain sense of adventure. Unlike me, he saw it as a chance to embrace the unknown, as an opportunity to become a bridge between the fairies and the dragons, to patch up a relationship that's been rocky at the best of times." Ta'ra hesitated. Her whiskers twitched. "But after what happened ... After the way Ta'lon treated me as an object after all this time. You know, destiny ... I'm starting to think there's no such thing. Does that make sense?"

I took a deep breath and thought upon her words for a moment. "But you must have seen other visions in your crystal. Other threads of the future."

"I never had a chance. I left my crystal alone that day, believing that my path had been set. But now I see what's happening with Seramina, and I just feel that some of you are accepting fate just *because* it's fate. Not choosing to side with uncertainty, because despite the certain aspect being the worst possible result, what could be scarier than the unknown?"

"I wish I could deal with uncertainty," I said.

Ta'ra paused as if to think for a moment. "You know, there's this saying we have in the Faerie Realm. My grandfather always said it to me, and now I'm telling it to you."

"What is it?"

Ta'ra let out a soft chirp which would have translated in the human language to a chuckle. "There's only one creature that can trick destiny, and that's a fairy. I guess that's what I did in the end ... I tricked destiny."

"That's one way of looking at it," I said. If only that were true – if it were possible to 'trick' destiny.

As we floated along within the sea of cats, our passageway forked off. The congregation continued along to the right, but Ta'ra pushed her way through the bodies towards the left. "It's this way ... Come on, Dragoncat."

I stopped, startled. As if I were just a rock in the river,

the cats flowed around me. "Where are you going, Ta'ra?"

"My crystal is this way; I can feel it calling. It never had a chance to ally itself with Dragonsbond Academy's Great Crystal before Lasinta broke it. It was always independent of it. Perhaps it was because it never entered the academy in the first place, but it never lost its life like the other crystals did."

"You mean to say—"

"Maybe you can find a way to talk to it too, Ben."

I looked back at Seramina, wondering if I needed to stay around her to stand guard. She moved forward with a sad and lonely gait, her eyes not seeming to want to look at anything but the floor. But she was here now, safe in the Versta Caverns, and I was sure that my friends would stop her from coming to any harm.

I followed Ta'ra, my true *companion*, slightly annoyed with myself that I was passing up the opportunity for a good meal. But that could wait, and the crystal couldn't.

26

TA'RA'S CRYSTAL

I let Ta'ra lead the way through the Versta Caverns, and I followed behind her closely. She moved with a fluid swaying motion, like a cat a following her nose, though I really knew it was the crystal guiding her inside her mind. Looking at her then, I couldn't believe she'd once been a fairy. The first time she'd left the Faerie Realm she'd always approached being a cat with caution, but this time she seemed to believe there was no turning back.

She had abandoned that lavender scent that she always used to carry for a start. As a fairy, she used to spray it on herself as a perfume, and then when she became a cat she would roll around for hours in a nearby lavender field. I'd told her numerous times that cats shouldn't smell like bees, but she'd never seemed to understand.

Now I couldn't have been more proud of her, and really I don't know what I'd been thinking with regard to

Esme. I didn't want to spend my life with a cat who was so entitled and bossy. Ta'ra was the right *companion* for me, and I didn't need another.

She and I could grow old together, and I could help her discover so many of the joys of being feline. Our species had the kind of freedom a fairy princess bound by court protocol could never quite appreciate. It seemed to me like royals had certain rules about how one should behave. The more money or status humans and fairies had, the more they seemed to become trapped by the expectations of society.

Cats have never had to worry about such things. So long as we had food and water in our bowls, and a soft surface to sleep on at night, then we could do whatever we pleased. Of course, we were wise enough to realise that we shouldn't do anything stupid. Waltzing right up to the kennel of a full-grown German shepherd and scratching it on the nose is, for example, off the cards for any of us who doesn't have a death wish.

As we walked, I found myself wondering what kind of magic Ta'ra's crystal would bestow upon her. Given that she used to be a fairy, I figured she might become a leaf mage just like Ange and Great Driar Brigel. The ability to summon vegetables out of the ground would be pretty useless for a cat, but still I might convince her to call upon some catnip from time to time. I just hoped she didn't revert to liking lavender.

The passageways seemed to get narrower as we went on. The crystals hugged the cavern walls so closely that I thought they might scratch us. Still, a good set of working whiskers guided me through unscathed, and we soon emerged into a much wider opening.

I smelled the earthy pond just before we rounded the corner, and then we emerged at quite a spectacle to behold. Ta'ra's crystal was lodged into the rock, water from the pond lapping against the base of it. There it stood upright, glowing brightly with images of the cats we had just separated from, emerging into a chamber wide and high enough to contain a small village. Through this, networks of crystals ran in spirals down columns set out across the length and breadth of the room. Their effect combined to fill the room with a gentle and comforting light.

The vision also showed the dragons coming out of another passageway, bringing great haunches of roast beef. These they placed on the floor, and the hundreds of cats pounced happily upon them. It made me sad for the meal I was missing or was about to miss. The crystal's depiction displayed the light in such a special way that the juices on the meat glistened. The mistress back home in South Wales would often place magazines on her coffee table with pictures on the front cover of delicious looking food that looked as impressive as the food in this vision. The crystal had made it look so appetising that I could almost smell it from here, and I could taste it in the juices forming at the back of my mouth.

The shallow pond surrounded Ta'ra's crystal, reflecting the light coming off it and from all the other smaller crystals that hugged the walls of the chamber like barnacles. This made the water's surface look like it was reflecting a thousand stars, twinkling to the cadence of its soft shimmer.

I was perhaps even more thirsty than I was hungry. It felt as if my legs were carrying me towards the water before my mind even told them to do so. I almost tripped over a loose rock on the way, but I didn't let it break my stride. Soon I had bounded up next to Ta'ra, who already had her snout in the water, lapping it up. I took a few mouthfuls myself, satisfied by the richness of it.

"What did I tell you," Ta'ra said. "No water tastes as good as cave water."

"You know," I said, "I think I now understand what you mean."

This particular water had more than just mineral earthiness to it. It was slightly warm and had an almost unnatural freshness. The magic made it feel as if it could heal forgotten injuries. I felt blood rushing to my cheeks, and a sting lifted from behind my eyes that I hadn't even realised was there.

Ta'ra turned her head up to the crystal. The images of our friends had now started to fade, replaced by pulses of white light, growing in intensity. Soon, I was treated to a familiar sight.

The crystal had lifted itself up out of the rock and it started to spin around on its longitudinal axis. Pride welled up in my heart, because this meant Ta'ra was about to receive her first gift, and her crystal had allowed me to be part of the show. It spoke in the voice of the crystals – soft, lilting, and female, with an accent not too different from a Welsh one.

"The cat who decided to become a fairy has reemerged from her dream," it said. "Alas, for the living the meaning of destiny is transient; only that which exists beyond time and space can truly understand its essence."

Ta'ra's cheeks had softened, and her mouth had become rounded, displaying her pink tongue. She gazed at her crystal, speechless. I backed away, deciding it better for her to have this moment undisturbed.

"It is clear now," her crystal continued, "that you have learned what you had to learn. You are neither fairy nor cat, but like all life just a lonely flame floating within a sea of darkness. Unlike the ones in your world, your flame is tough to extinguish. Yet it easy to forget or take for granted. When you focus on the darkness, you forget the fact you have a light at all. But it can always be found, and it can guide you. Remember this, and it doesn't matter what or who you are. Only the essence of your existence matters, and it will keep you whole."

Ta'ra lowered her head. Her eyes glinted in the reflection of the water, and then she closed them. "I guess that is true," she said. "I am not my past, and I am not my future."

"There are forces in the worlds that will urge you to forget that. But you have powers of your own, and they will serve you in the time yet to come."

The crystal paused. As if recognising it wasn't her turn to speak, Ta'ra said nothing. I said nothing either – this was Ta'ra's place now. I didn't even need to be here. All I could hear was the gentle lapping of the water, the humming of the crystals, and lost echoes of happenings beyond the chamber's walls.

"Now, Fairycat," the crystal continued, "it is time for your gift."

I heard Ta'ra's breath catch in her throat. "My only gift?" she muttered.

"You only need one, for you have everything else you need within. Now you are ready to receive your staff."

Before Ta'ra had a chance to utter another word, there came a sudden splash from the water. Coming out of nowhere, a giant white hand leapt out – a staff bearer summoned from the spaces between the dimensions. It had its fingers and thumb wrapped around a staff unlike any I'd ever seen before. Because this staff was not made of solid matter, but rather glimmers of golden light that seemed to rotate around absent spaces. It took me only a moment to realise the whole thing was made of countless specks of fairy dust, dancing around in a focused pattern to give the staff its form.

I smelled honey, and pollen, and the rich freshness of the Faerie Realm.

"It's ..." Ta'ra began, then her voice trailed off.

"You have known this magic since birth," Ta'ra's crystal said. "There is no need for you to learn another magic when in service as a dragon rider."

"I don't know what to say," Ta'ra said.

"Say nothing, and just accept the gift."

Ta'ra did exactly as she had been told. She opened her eyes and her mouth to accept the staff bearer's offering as it swept before her. Her jaws clenched around the staff, which glimmered, and then from the lake came a flash of yellow.

The water in front of us turned to steam, and out of that steam arose a plume of butterflies in myriad colours and patterns. Ta'ra giggled in a very fairy type of way, and I felt the urge to chase after a particularly large looking cabbage white butterfly.

But the crystal pulsed bright white again, pulling my attention back towards it. This time its words were for me.

"Now, Dragoncat," it said. "Your *companion* wasn't the only one who came here with a purpose, for you too are lost and need to find your way."

The crystal's words caused me to freeze in my tracks. I hadn't actually realised the truth of what it said until it had said it.

"Alas, we need to go to another place. For this journey you will need to travel alone."

All of a sudden, the scene before me was flooded with light. This soon faded and I found myself alone in pitch darkness. Or at least I thought I was alone, until I heard the voice of *Cana Dei*.

27

DARKNESS AND LIGHT

There was nothing in the place the crystal had transported me to, only darkness so thick that I couldn't even imagine shapes within it. I tried to take a step forwards, but it felt like trying to wade through honey that had only recently lost its solidity. Even the air felt so heavy that a single breath felt like sucking in water. Then I smelled that same yucky scent I'd first encountered in the Ghost Realm, redolent of yeast extract, and I knew *Cana Dei* was close.

It's only an illusion, I told myself. *The crystals wouldn't take me to a place where I could die.* But had the crystal even taken me to this place, or had that been just an illusion? Perhaps everything that had brought me to this moment in time – to this unceasing blackness – had been the work of *Cana Dei*.

I listened, hoping to hear that soft Welsh-like lilting voice that I'd missed for so long. It had guided me so many times that when Salanraja's and my crystal had broken, I'd felt lost. I guessed I hadn't stopped feeling lost, despite Ta'ra turning up and bringing me comfort. I just had no idea where to go next.

The voice of *Cana Dei* rumbled through the darkness. I couldn't determine its direction; it came from all places at once.

"Dragoncat," it said, "so much has happened. But you have been ignoring my voice, blocking it out somehow. Now there is so much to discuss."

"I have no business with you," I said. "Only with the crystals."

"Oh, so that it is how you came to be here. You know, for some reason the crystals have given me a path right into the essence of your being. I could reach in from here and suck your soul out of the Fifth Dimension right now, though I won't. You may still prove useful to me."

But I hadn't been brought here to speak to *Cana Dei*, I was sure. I had ears only for the crystals.

"*Why did you bring me here?*" I asked in my mind, speaking to it in the same way that I'd spoken to it before.

For a moment I got no response, only silence. I could feel *Cana Dei's* presence nearby, tugging on my fur like a balloon charged with static. I could also feel my pulse thrumming through the veins in every single muscle of my body.

Suddenly, just in front of me, came a flash of white. Then before me hovered a crystal, floating in mid-air, or at least what I thought it was mid-air because I couldn't see the ground. It spun on its longitudinal axis. It wasn't Ta'ra's crystal but my own crystal as I'd first encountered it when it had given me the gift of speaking all languages. In other words, it didn't look grey and lifeless anymore, but instead shone with buoyant vibrance.

"Why did you bring me here?" I asked again.

The reply didn't come from in front but behind me, and it spoke in the deep, rumbling timbre of *Cana Dei*.

"A brave choice for the crystals, to face their nemesis," it said. I turned around to see the dark swirling orb hovering there. White flares danced in and out of its surface, giving it substance. "If you'd only give me an opening. Access to the Ninth Dimension. Then I could destroy you all."

"There is no Ninth Dimension," the crystal replied out loud. Although technically it didn't have any volume at all, since all this was happening within the realm of my own mind.

"So you say," *Cana Dei* said, "and so you would have every single creature that you allow access to your magic believe. Even the immortals think that it all ends at the void at the end of time and space. And I am after all the most powerful of the immortals to roam the lands. But where, tell me, does the magic of the crystals reside? Because aren't you after all the overseers of everything? You aren't just the crystals, are you? They are a conduit to another plane, where you, whatever you are, exist."

"We aren't here to discuss our essence." The crystal pulsed with light more rapidly than before as it spoke, giving the impression of being slightly aggravated.

"Then I shall taunt you no longer," *Cana Dei* said. "Because I am intrigued as to what purpose you can give to the Dragoncat that might involve me. Why, indeed, did you bring him before me?"

Cana Dei fell silent, and I waited for my crystal to speak. While *Cana Dei's* voice had sent my heart palpitating in fear, now my crystal's voice seemed to soothe it. But already the dark force's intervention had caused me to start to wonder: were the crystals as it had suggested just communication channels of another species that was manipulating us all? Perhaps their intention wasn't as pure as I'd always believed.

"Dragoncat," my crystal said, "I brought you here to help you find your way. What is it that you seek?"

I stopped to think only for a moment. The question hadn't been clear in my mind up until that very point. All our efforts to keep Seramina locked away, the cats and the dragons that were meant to guard her – somehow, I didn't believe that we could prevent that terrifying scene where she plunged her staff into the ground, rending it apart and summoning the demons up from the earth. After all, it was the only possible outcome we'd ever seen of the crystals' premonitions, and the visions of her future we'd viewed that time we'd visited the Ghost Realm. We seemed only to be delaying the inevitable.

"How can we stop Seramina from destroying the worlds?" I asked. "And if there is no way of doing it, what is the point of even trying? So far, all the possible paths lead to the same place."

The crystal pulsed with energy as if to answer, but instead *Cana Dei* cut in. "Cats, dragons, humans, dogs. You're all the same. You think you can find a way to control the future. But ultimately all life ends in the same place, in soil and dust."

"So it's futile?" I asked. "We should just make the most of the lives we have left and enjoy ourselves? In that case, please take me back to the Fourth Dimension where I came from, because I want one last meal of smoked salmon before it all ends. Oh, and send Ta'ra there, because I want to give her a chance to try it too."

"Of course it is futile," *Cana Dei* said. "I will control you all."

"Except there is another path," my crystal said. "But it will involve a great sacrifice."

"You cannot stop it," *Cana Dei* said. "I will control the souls of all eventually. Unless ..."

You could cut the silence that fell with a claw. It was so prominent, I felt it in my whiskers. My eyelids twitched.

"Yes," my crystal said. "Unless ..." An image formed on its facets in grey and purple.

"You can't possibly mean it. Dragoncat ... A sacrifice. No, he's still young and supple. I could mould him into whatever I please. Yes, he could become just as powerful as the teenager."

I started to feel a sense that I'd entered a part of a trade, and I didn't feel particularly comfortable about it.

"But it will buy them time," my crystal said. "It will give them another chance to find a way to finally win ..."

In the vision within its facets, I could now make out rocky shapes. The landscape was barren, and I could see that yucky purple mist rising up from the cracks in the ground.

"Yet no matter how much the creatures of the world struggle to survive," *Cana Dei* said, "they will eventually meet their untimely end. They can deviate from destiny only for so long."

"And yet they will fight, and they will sacrifice to live better lives."

Humanoid shapes started to form out of the blurs within the rocks. I could make out a hovel, and a girl with flowing silver hair standing in front of it. She held a glowing white staff, and the view spun to show the six warlocks clutching their own staffs at the ready. Lasinta led the warlocks, and she took a stride so that she was ahead of the rest of them. Her ancient eyebrows furrowed, and I could see the menace in her eyes.

We were back to the familiar prophecy, and I had an eerie sensation that this time it was going to end with a dark twist. Seramina's eyes burned with crimson fire, and a future version of me stepped onto the scene just beneath her knees.

"Dragoncat, this is your moment of sacrifice," my crystal said.

"I see," *Cana Dei* said. "Most intriguing ..."

In the vision, my fur lost its brilliant vibrancy, and faded from amber to a dull grey. Purple gas seeped up out of the ground around my depicted form, trickling into its nostrils. The view spun again to show my eyes blazing with that same deep fire. Then when my staff bearer came out of the darkness, it too had the same purple hue as the atmosphere.

"You are the only one the teenager trusts," my crystal said. "She will only let her guard down for you, and so this is the only possible thread that remains."

"Yet still, you will delay the inevitable," *Cana Dei* said.

Seramina's gaze was focused on the warlocks, as they wove their staffs through the air to summon great mist dragons into the sky. She lifted her staff into the air, and its magic sucked the darkness away from the scene. Then would come the moment when she would break the worlds.

Except my future form already had its staff in its mouth, the crystal glowing with a brilliant intensity of its own. Out came a bright beam of light that hit Seramina right in the chest.

I didn't need to see what happened to Seramina next. I could all but imagine how she would crumble to ash, her life dissipating into the void. And yet I would have saved the world. But still as the view turned once again, I could see how the fire still burned at the back of my eyes, and my fur never regained its normal colour.

A dragon swooped down and landed on the ground and I saw it to be Salanraja – except something within her had changed too. All along the length of her body, her spikes had changed to long purple crystals. She was glimmering with a magic of her own, and her eyes burned with that same eldritch intensity as mine.

"That is the sacrifice?" *Cana Dei* asked. "You would take her life and give me the cat and his dragon?"

"Dragoncat must choose," my crystal said. "And this moment will be presented only once. Either the young warlock breaks the worlds, or the cat will lose himself to you forever."

"You can rule, immortal Dragoncat," *Cana Dei* said. "Eventually I can teach you to break the worlds in your own way. Then the demons – the armies of Ammit – will be yours to command. Yours and mine, that is. In truth, we are all the same."

My skin was itching underneath my fur, as if I'd suddenly been attacked by a swarm of fleas. I felt dirty, and I felt evil. But at the same time, I realised we had no choice. So far, we'd only been presented with one option for the future, and now we had another. I would lose myself to the darkness, and I'd sacrifice a good friend. But what other choice did I have?

"I'll do it," I said. "If I can save the worlds and make it better for everyone else. I will do what needs to be done."

"Despite what you will have to sacrifice?" my crystal asked, and its voice no longer sounded soft and lilting. Now the voice had a hard edge to it, almost as if it represented the choice I would have to make.

"Despite that," I said. "I must ..."

"Then good luck, Dragoncat," *Cana Dei* said. "I shall watch your progress with interest, though don't think I'll make any concessions should you fail to make your choice."

This time, there was no light that preluded my vision's fade to darkness, and the absence of that light seemed to last an awful long time. Eventually I found myself back in the same chamber, gazing up at Ta'ra's crystal and sitting next to her.

All of a sudden these caverns didn't feel quite as safe as they had done before.

28

POSSIBILITIES

I was silent on the way to meet our friends, which wasn't hard admittedly since Ta'ra clearly wanted to talk. She nattered on about how pleased she was that she'd gained her fairy magic back again, and that she'd known she'd made the right choice. Honestly, I didn't register even half of it because the obvious dilemma was spinning around in my head.

Could I really do what my crystal had revealed I could do? To end Seramina's life just like that? One thing was for sure, the crystal and *Cana Dei* had both been confident that Seramina would break the worlds, which meant it was futile to keep her here, because something would eventually force her to leave. It was only a matter of time.

As we walked down the passageway, the crystals lit the way in their normal fashion, seeming to grow in size as we approached the larger room. The caverns also widened out, and I could smell the scent of chargrilled beef that should have been enticing, but I'd lost my appetite.

Meanwhile, I planned to keep the matter at hand as secret as I could, not telling anyone about it if possible. Of course, given how much it occupied my mind, it was impossible to keep it from Salanraja. She'd been previously absent from my mind, spending some time talking with Matharon and the other Guardians. But once she saw the terrible images in my head, she latched right onto them.

"It seems you've been presented with quite a dilemma," she said.

"Salanraja, you must promise to tell no one about this. If anyone finds out, they might tell Seramina, and then we won't have a chance of stopping her if she destroys the world."

"But you won't just end her, you'll end up sacrificing yourself, and then I'll have to fly in and try to stop you. And either I'll have to end your life – or you, or at least your body, will end mine."

"No," I said. *"Cana Dei will inhabit your mind too. It seems that it will take advantage of our bond and use that to turn you into its servant. And then your horns and your spikes will turn into dark crystals, and they'll smell like rotten vegetable juice."*

"And you're okay with that?"

"Of course I'm not okay with it. But I don't see any other choice. Do you?"

"I really don't like this, Bengie. There must be another way. I just can't understand why the crystals would present

this to you. So far everything that they've done for us has been noble. But this ... This is something else."

"Maybe the crystals aren't as noble as we've always thought. Perhaps they have a dark side, too."

"Or it's a trick of Cana Dei. *Did you ever think about that? What if it's using your own mind and your own beliefs to manipulate you?"*

"Why then would the crystals give Ta'ra her gift? You're not going to tell me that Cana Dei *managed to somehow find a staff for her with fairy magic, because I can't believe that."*

"I don't know, Bengie. But don't do anything until we've had a chance to think this over. There has to be another way ..."

"Just promise you won't tell anyone, Salanraja. Because you've gone behind my back too many times before, and if you do it this time I'll never forgive you."

Though I expected her to hesitate, she replied immediately. *"Okay, I promise."*

"You promise what?"

"I promise I won't go behind your back about this matter. I won't tell anyone. I know that it's better not to in such a circumstance. This time, I know you're not just being stupid like the other times; this is a difficult situation. Really, I don't know what we're going to do, but whatever it is, I'm sure you'll make the best choice."

"I hope so," I said, but at the same time I had a foreboding feeling that I didn't have a choice at all.

29

PROPOSAL

I would have thought things couldn't have got any worse that day, but it seemed fate wasn't on my side.

As soon as I arrived in the large chamber where everyone had gathered, I wasn't quite watching where I was going and stumbled right into Rine's leg. He was wearing the most sickening cologne. This time he didn't have his arm around Bellari's shoulder; rather he had stepped away from her, and she was watching him with rapt fascination.

It wasn't just her own attention that was focused on Rine; every eye in the massive chamber was on him. The human dragon riders sitting on ledges, the dragons who had emerged from the mouths of the winding passageways, hundreds of cats standing stock-still as if they had heard a hawk, and Matharon and his guardians with their glowing eyes peering out from openings in the upper walls.

A pile of meat stood uneaten in the centre of this

giant chamber, and besides it lay an even larger pile of bones.

Rine looked down at me, a smirk on his face. "Oh there you are, Ben. I thought you were going to miss the moment."

"The moment?" I asked.

"Please, there's no time now. I need to stay in the flow while I have everyone's attention."

"What the whiskers is this, Rine?" I asked. "Because I'm really not in the mood ..."

"Just let me ..." His voice trailed off and he got down on one knee. At the same time, he reached into a pocket of his robe and pulled out a box wrapped in velvet. This he opened to reveal a ring, fashioned from old bits of twine.

"Oh no," I said. But Rine didn't seem to hear me.

"I'm sorry, I've not had a chance to get a proper ring," Rine said. "But I can once this whole thing's over. I just thought we should make the most of the moments we have together. Just in case, well, you know ... There's so much danger nowadays, and I just wanted you to know—"

Bellari took a step towards him, cutting him off. "Just stop bumbling, darling, and get on with it." The gaze that she held on Rine was filled with anticipation.

"Buttercup ..." Rine continued, "I love you, and I've been thinking."

He stopped and for the first time his face went red. "Bellari, I—"

"Oh, Rine," Bellari said, her cheeks an equal crimson. "Just say it."

"Bellari, I—" he stopped himself, took a deep breath. The colour drained from his face. Then he reached out and took Bellari's hand. "All I wanted to ask is, will you marry me?"

Bellari let out a squeal of delight. Then she leant over and kissed Rine on the cheek. "Of course I will, silly. Here, let me try it on."

She held out her hand, and Rine slipped the ring on her finger. From further into the chamber someone shouted, "Whoop, whoop," and I turned in astonishment to see Ange clapping her hands. She wasn't with the big-footed oaf, Kamino; the muscular teenager stood leaning against a column a good several yards away, watching the newly engaged couple as they embraced.

I didn't want anything more to do with Rine and Bellari right now, so I went over to give Ange a piece of my mind. She looked down at Palimali who lay sleeping at her feet and then turned her head to me.

"Ben," she said. "Where did you get off to? You cats have a strange habit of disappearing."

I didn't want to tell her about my encounter with *Cana Dei*, but I guess I did have some news. "We went to see Ta'ra's crystal, and she got her magic and her staff for the first time."

Ange's face lit up. "She did? I thought the crystals were—"

"Not Ta'ra's crystal," I said. "It's been here all along, since she never had a chance to take it back to Dragonsbond Academy. It turns out it wasn't affected like all the other crystals when the Great Crystal broke."

"That's wonderful," Ange said. "It really is."

"Anyway …" I looked back to see that Rine and Bellari had now started to kiss. "What's the meaning of this? You're not meant to be supporting them as a couple."

"What? Why not? They're good together … Rine came and asked if I'd mind, and I told him I wouldn't. We're friends after all, aren't we?"

"And what about Kamino?" I said. "I thought you were with him to try and make Rine jealous."

"Not at all. I just thought it might make it a little easier for him if I spent some time with him. He really liked Bellari, as so many of the guys do. It just wasn't meant to be, though."

"His feet are too big to be in a relationship," I said. "No one can trust him."

Ange laughed. "What is it with you and big feet?"

"Everything … Anyway …"

I gazed over at the pile of meat, considering that I should eat something. Ta'ra had already found her way over and was working her way around a juicy steak. Some of the other cats watched her passively, and a couple even went over to eat with her. I turned back to Ange and meowed. She smiled and petted me gently on the head.

"You know, I've realised something recently, Ben," she said. "I'm just not interested in boys in the way that most girls are. Things are a little different for me, you see."

"You've said that you'd rather focus on your studies ..."

"That's, um, one way of putting it ..." She looked as if she wanted to add something, but Esme abruptly came over, trailed by Geni and Rex. The Abyssinian looked as if she had a purpose.

"And where, Dragoncat, may I ask have you been?"

I raised up my head and looked as proud as I could. "A mission of prime importance."

"One that I didn't have to know about, I figure," she looked back at Ta'ra with an expression of distaste.

"You don't need to know about every single movement I make, do you? I'm a cat, and I'm meant to be free."

"I just hope you weren't off causing trouble." She sniffed at my tail. "I smell something different about you. Like, fairies ... Are they here?"

"No, there's no fairies. Just – it's none of your business, Esme, okay? I'm allowed to have thoughts of my own, aren't I?"

I hissed at her, and Esme hissed right back. Behind her Geni and Rex had their hackles up, but they didn't look as if they wanted to join in a scrap should one occur. It might involve magic and I guessed neither of them knew how to use that yet.

I turned around, right into the wet nose of Max. He had a shank of beef in his jaws which he dropped it right at my feet. It looked nibbled around edges.

"You looked hungry, Ben," he panted in the dog language. "I brought you some food."

I looked down at it in disgust. "I'm not going to eat that now it's been in *your* mouth."

"Why not?" he asked, then started to bark. "This is perfectly good meat."

"Look, I didn't ask for it, so leave me alone."

He blinked at me confusedly, then he pushed his nose forward and it looked as if he was going to try and lick me. I don't like to have to tell animals twice, and so I reached out a paw and scratched at his nose.

He whimpered and then scampered off, crying, "Warg, warg, fierce meanie Dragoncat warg."

I decided it was better to find some more sombre company. I passed Aleam leaning over to stroke Ta'ra, who had just fallen asleep a short distance away from the pile of meat. I soon found Seramina, sitting in a shadowed alcove by herself. She had her staff laid down by her feet and her eyes looked as grey as her father's had been.

"Ben ..." she said as I lay down beneath her.

"Seramina," I said.

Silence passed between us for several moments, then she nodded over at Rine and Bellari and said, "I guess I should be happy for them. I liked Rine and Ange, but she told me that he's not for her."

"You have no need to feel anything," I said. "You've been through a lot lately."

"I guess ..." Seramina's gaze roved over to a point where several cats had clustered together, grooming themselves. "Ben, can I ask something?"

"Go on ..."

"Do you think we can prevent me from meeting the

warlocks? I mean we've brought all the cats here, and they're going to become dragon riders. And Matharon told me before that he's going to do everything possible to protect me. But I can't stop wondering – can we stop what the crystals predicted?"

I looked into her eyes, searching for signs of the fires burning inside. But they remained colourless and sober.

"Tell me, Seramina," I said softly, so no one could hear. "Have you continued to commune with *Cana Dei* since we've been here?"

Her eyes narrowed. "No. I mean, yes, I hear it sometimes. It tries to talk to me. But I've been ignoring it, I think."

"And what does it keep saying?"

"That the time is coming soon, that we will have to leave. It tells me I can't change anything. I've been trying to ignore it, Ben. I really have."

I growled and decided that I didn't want to continue this subject anymore. I turned back to the cats, who carried on with their grooming as if oblivious to the danger we were in. Once I'd been like that – a feline free spirit without a care in the world.

"I *hope* that we can protect you from that confrontation with the warlocks," I said, and I don't know how genuine I sounded.

Seramina had no time for any more questions, anyway, because Matharon flew down from his place in the upper walls and into the centre of the chamber. The cats there parted to make way for him, and he landed just short of the food, his tail resting on the discarded bones.

His voice boomed out, echoing against the walls of the chamber. "We have gathered here for a momentous occasion," he said. "And now it is time for our brave new feline riders to bond with their dragons. Therefore, let the ceremonies begin."

30

CEREMONY

The soon-to-be feline dragon riders lined up in rows of around twenty, Rex and Geni front and centre. As they did so, the dwarf dragons flowed out from the corridors, forming a queue in front of them. Alongside the sweet and musty scent given off by the crystals, which lit the chamber in a spectrum of colours, came the reek of sulphur. Soon enough there were sufficient dragons in the room to make it smell like a volcano. I imagined for a moment I was in the Seventh Dimension, for I'd visited there once. But unlike the searing heat of the magmatic realm, this chamber had a humid warmth to it.

The giant bronze dragon Matharon stood between the rows of cats and dragons. As the dragons rolled in, he watched them with apparent pride. They were less than half the height of normal dragons; fate had delivered a large batch of dwarf dragons to Matharon this year. I hadn't even considered how odd it was until that moment that there were no normal sized dragons.

But they say dragons draw their magic from the crystals, which is why they can't breathe fire within the Versta Caverns. Thus the crystals must have had a reason for this anomaly. I figured it was all a part of the grand plan of theirs, but I just wished I knew what that was.

"Matharon has told us that he wants to accelerate the process of training these cats as mages," Salanraja said. *"He thinks that he can get them working with magic in a few months."*

"But they need staffs," I pointed out.

"Of course they do, but our loyal leader says he has hope. He has worked long enough now in these caverns that he can tell if the crystals are planning something."

"And they can't even use magic in the Versta Caverns," I said, *"so they won't be able to train here."*

"I know ... But they'll train outside, and sleep in the caverns. It's such a safe place for them, when you think it through. I doubt Captain Alliander and the rest of the White Mages even realise we're here. Each dragon rider will need to pass a test of their own, but by the end of it we could have a force that would pose a challenge for the warlocks."

I contemplated this for a moment. It made me wonder if the crystals had presented the dilemma about the choice I might have to make just to play for time. Perhaps this occurrence could create another thread in the future of possibilities. In my mind's eye, I imagined how a portal might open just as Seramina was about to thrust her staff into the ground, from which an army of dragon riding cats would sweep out. Seramina would laugh, and Lasinta and the other warlocks would look up in fear, and then they would flee. Because if one mighty Bengal could kill Astravar, just imagine what two hundred magic-wielding cats could do.

But this theory had a problem of its own: though *Cana Dei* was unable to cast magic in these caverns, it could still listen in to our conversations by reading our minds. We didn't have the advantage of secrecy from our enemy whilst planning our tactics. *Cana Dei* would automatically know about any move that we made.

I've heard economists in the human realm of the Fourth Dimension have a similar theory of their own. They call it the Efficient Market Hypothesis, the idea that you can't predict the tides of the stock market, because by the time a trader receives news of something that might make them their weight in gold, the market has already adjusted to account for the new information. In other words, by the time anyone receives news about a worthwhile investment, it's already too late to act. Alas, that was also the case with *Cana Dei*. It was always one step ahead of us.

Any dragon rider who had already been initiated stood behind the cats, so we could watch the ceremony from afar. I stood on the left of Seramina, near Esme, Ta'ra and Max. The four students and Aleam stood on Seramina's right, looking on with reverent gazes.

We were the audience, there to cheer and applaud each new Initiate as they prepared for their first flight. It was going to be a long day, because apparently two hundred and twenty-two cats needed to bond with their dragons. Matharon would have to announce each one.

But first he had to make a speech. Though the cats stayed in their places, they wouldn't stop meowing. Some of them wanted food, despite having eaten a good meal just an hour ago. Matharon let out a harsh cough, and when that did little to quieten the cats, out came a mighty roar. It was so loud that it shook the cavern, and perhaps even dislodged a few crystals. It also stunned the cats into silence.

"Very good, very good," Matharon said. "I'm happy to see that I've not lost my touch despite my old age."

"*What a legend,*" Salanraja said.

"*I thought you detested him,*" I objected.

"*I never said that ... I said I feared him. But that's what makes him so mighty.*"

"*Just shut up, I want to listen to his speech,*" I said.

"*Yeah, right you do. You just don't want me nattering inside your head.*"

One thing was sure, Matharon certainly liked to talk. His words rumbled on throughout the cavern about the greatness of Bestian Academy. It was unfortunate, he claimed, that these dragons couldn't bond with the cats at Dragonsbond Academy, as was the custom. But perhaps this could be a sign of traditions changing. What better way to initiate new dragon riders than to send them to the freezing mountains to test their mettle.

Admittedly, though Matharon droned on, his way of speaking wasn't boring. The way he used his voice and the way he ducked his head around in the rhythm of his words made him quite entertaining. Still, I found myself letting out a few yawns – it's a cat's nature after staying in a place so long to do so, and my legs were telling me they wanted to fold up so I could go to sleep on the ground. But I didn't; something within me was telling me that I needed to stay alert.

Everyone's gaze was so securely fastened on Matharon that I'm not sure anyone noticed the purple glimmer in the crystals. After all it only happened for a fraction of a moment. A shudder went down my spine.

"*Yes, Dragoncat,*" *Cana Dei* said in my mind. "*I am here.*"

The glimmer came again. It was just a brief flicker only microseconds long. But still I saw it, and I began to smell rotten vegetable juice upon the air.

I growled and I shouted, "Danger!" as loud as I could in the human language.

But I didn't have Matharon's vocal cords, and my words were lost within his bass timbre.

"Danger!" I called again, and I tried it in the dog language, barking.

Max turned to me and bared his teeth to tell me to shut up. He was still angry with me for swiping him on the nose.

Seramina also seemed to notice my alarm. She turned down at me and said softly, "We can't stop this, Ben. It's destiny."

Her gaze looked vacant. Again, I looked for the fire burning at the back of her eyes. It wasn't there, and the expression on her face displayed a reluctant acceptance.

She looked as if she'd given up fighting and would march to whatever tune fate resolved to play for her. Now there was no turning back.

The glimmer in the crystals came one more time, and they filled with energy for longer, suffusing the cavern with a grim light. Purple gas seeped up from the ground, just as it had days ago when our new Great Crystal had broken.

Matharon halted his speech, and he craned his giant head upwards. His bulk cast an ominous shadow. "What is going on? This isn't normal—"

His last word hung in the air, vibrating as if someone had struck a tuning fork against the bare rock. It took me a moment to realise that everyone had frozen – Aleam had his staff drawn, pushed forwards, one foot suspended off the ground. Max had his lips curled back, his teeth showing, and his mouth shaped into a wide bark. Esme had her staff in her mouth, and she had turned to face Seramina. But it seemed that she had cast her magic far too late.

Just like at Dragonsbond Academy, Seramina held her staff in the air, forbidden magic pulsing out of the crystal in flashes of brilliant white.

"This is impossible," I said to Seramina. "Magic in here is forbidden by the crystals."

"Unless they deign to allow it," she replied. "Have you ever stopped to consider that these crystals might not actually be on our side?"

My breath caught in my throat, as the realisation rushed through my mind. "In that case ... These caverns are the most dangerous of places we could have brought you to."

Seramina seemed not to hear, or if she did, she didn't care. "You are destined to come with me, Ben. You've been in every single prophecy I've seen, and I know that you've also been interfacing *Cana Dei*."

It's a horrible thing to say, but part of me wished at that moment that Seramina's magic had frozen me in time along with my comrades. I didn't want to be an agent in Seramina's destiny. I didn't want to play my part in stopping her from destroying the worlds.

But at the same time, I knew I had no other choice.

The air hummed with a thousand harmonies as the fabric of space-time in front of Seramina tore open. A portal appeared before her into darkness. Fringed with white light, it beckoned us onwards.

Without hesitation, Seramina stepped through.

If I had hesitated a moment longer the portal would have sealed before me, and she would have gone on to destroy the worlds alone. But my body told me where it needed to go before my mind even caught up with it. I bounded through, tumbling on the other side over the hard cold stones.

I wasn't the only one to step through, because I heard another form slink over the threshold behind me. It was only once the portal had closed that I caught sight of Ta'ra's bright green eyes.

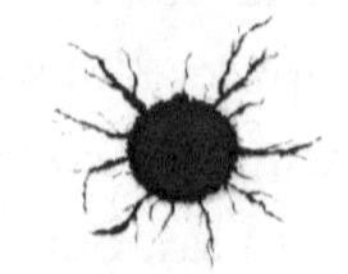

INTERLUDE
CANA DEI

Well, well, well, well, well.

I've been watching the events unfold through all your minds. From the Ghost Realm, I have seen history's conflicts across the annals of time, and I have never been so intrigued.

Haven't events taken an unsurprising turn? My dear Seramina, my powerful young warlock, you seem to have realised the part you must play in this stage production. And then there's your Dragoncat, your most trusted friend, the one who must always turn traitor.

Yet still the question remains ... Will the Dragoncat step up to his chosen role and take the young girl's life?

Oh, Seramina, Seramina, perhaps I should warn you. If I were not immortal, if I had but a limited time, perhaps I would. But the cat could equally well break the worlds, and I'm beginning to believe that he would do it better than you would.

Dragoncat, can you remember when Astravar turned you feral for a while? It worked rather well, don't you think? I can all but see it happening again, because there's a certain spirit living within you, one of a fighting beast.

Sadly, I know as little as either of you do about which of these two preordained paths destiny will choose. But if I were to hedge my bets, I would say that the Dragoncat would make the deliciously unsavoury and necessary choice. It's in his nature after all; cats weren't designed at the end of the day to preserve human lives. They're only meant to look after themselves.

That's what you would have said before this all started, wouldn't you, Dragoncat? Before that 'evil' warlock pulled you out of your comfortable home and into this fraught and dangerous life.

Do not worry yourself, Ammit. I know if it goes this way you will have to wait longer to release your armies. And they look magnificent lined up on that one craggy plateau, the whole of the Seventh Dimension condensed into one place.

Yes, it might take more time. But it will happen eventually.

If Dragoncat decides to submit to me, that is. Then I might even turn him into a demon cat himself.

But if he cannot do it, if he lets the young warlock plunge her staff into the fabric of oblivion and release the magic that will eventually unite the dimensions, then you will have your moment very soon, I promise you.

Very soon indeed.

31

WAITING

A light came on in the darkness.

Soon this erupted into a brightly burning flame. It hovered at the tip of Seramina's staff, emitting a furious heat and casting harsh shadows across her face. The reflection of the fire in her eyes made it looks as if they were burning with *Cana Dei*. But it was only a trick of the light.

I felt the hackles shoot up along the back of my neck, as I thought she had decided to eliminate Ta'ra and me. Had she somehow learned of my intended treachery and decided that she needed to act now to preserve her life?

She turned and thrust her staff forwards. The blaze wrapped itself into a ball and shot off a short distance. It flared upon impact, displaying the shadows of a stone hearth, a neatly stacked pile of firewood beneath it. This burst into flames, filling the room with a warm orange light.

We were in a small cabin by the looks of it, with

wooden walls that looked eaten with woodworm and windows that had been completely boarded up. It was sparsely furnished, with just a single bed clothed with a dusty blanket, a rickety looking trestle table, a few even more wobbly stools strewn around, and a few wall shelves containing a selection of cast iron pots and pans for the hearth. Everything looked so old here. Abandoned. A door stood closed on the wall opposite the fireplace, and it looked like it didn't have a lock.

In a way, it seemed strange not to see cobwebs, but there was something in the air that told me that not even spiders could live here. It took me a while, amidst the mildew and the fresh smell of woodsmoke to detect that acrid stench of rotten vegetable juice. It permeated the place, coming from the tiny tendrils of purple mist that seeped up between the stones on the ground. We were in the Darklands, the lair of the warlocks, and this was clearly the hovel where Seramina would make her stand.

She pulled a stool over to the fireplace and sat down upon it. One hand she used to hold her staff against the ground, whilst her other supported her forehead as she leaned forwards. She kept her eyes on the floor, not seeming to want to acknowledge my or Ta'ra's presence.

I walked over to my *companion*, who had already taken the most favourable spot by the fire. She lay beside it grooming her fur. I spoke to her in the cat language.

"You shouldn't have come, Ta'ra."

"Why the whiskers not?" she said. "You need protection from yourself, Ben."

"And what is that supposed to mean?"

Ta'ra looked up at Seramina. "Just go and talk to her, Ben. Maybe we can work things out before it even has to start. If we can just find a way to *trick* destiny."

I wondered if she had an inkling of what I would have to do. But that was surely impossible – I'd seen no sign of her communing with *Cana Dei* in any way. She had not touched either dark or white magic in her life, which seemed to be the two pathways to it. The only soul I'd told was Salanraja, and this time I truly believed her when she'd said she'd keep it secret. Even if she hadn't, I could see no reason why she'd even think of telling Ta'ra.

What I hadn't quite worked out, and I was in such a flummoxed state of mind I hadn't even questioned it that much at the time, was why the crystals hadn't frozen Ta'ra like they had the others in the Versta Caverns. I guess once the former Cat Sidhe realised what I was up to then she'd try to stop me. If, as Seramina had proposed, the crystals weren't on our side after all, then that would make it a lot harder for me, making it all the more probable that Seramina would tear a rift open in the ground and summon the demons from the Seventh Dimension.

I stalked over to Seramina and placed myself right underneath her gaze, then I looked up at her with wide eyes and meowed.

She turned her head away. "Really, I'm not in the mood, Ben."

"I just thought that you might appreciate me on your lap ..."

"No!" she snapped back, and I bristled. But I stood my ground.

I started to roam around Seramina's perimeter, sniffing the stool and the flagstones, and then Seramina's leg. She no longer smelled of snowdrop perfume. In all honesty, she smelled as if she hadn't washed for a couple of days.

"I wonder who used to live here," I said.

"I don't know. Maybe no one."

"No, it smells of humans," I said. "Maybe it once belonged to one of the warlocks."

"I really don't care," Seramina said. "Please, just leave me alone. I want to spend these final moments in peace and quiet. I want to remember …" She trailed off. "I want to remember the good person I always dreamed of being."

Her voice grew strained and her eyes a little red at the bottom. I expected to see tears, yet there were none. The crystal on her staff glowed purple for a moment and I saw the flash of *Cana Dei* in her eyes. It seemed almost a threat that if I tried anything she'd overpower me. I had to be careful what I said if I wanted to keep her trust.

I decided to try a different tack.

"Look, you don't have to do this, Seramina," I said.

"You know that I do. We've all seen the premonitions, and you know as well as I do that all paths lead to here."

"No, you don't. You just think you do because everything so far has been saying you must. But you can make a choice. It's like Ta'ra was telling me before – you can find a way to trick destiny."

"I know the saying," Seramina said. "I've read the

books, you know. Only fairies can find a way to trick destiny. But I'm not a fairy, and neither is Ta'ra anymore, either. So I guess we're stuck."

Her words were laced with spite, as if she wanted to hurt my *companion*. Wisely, Ta'ra didn't pay her any heed, continuing to groom herself as if she didn't have a care in the world.

"So that's it then?" I said. "We just wait here and let fate take its course?"

"It won't be long now," Seramina said. "*Cana Dei* has told me exactly when to expect the warlocks."

"And when will that be?"

"Soon," Seramina said. "Now if you don't want me to perform another regrettable action this day, I suggest you leave me in peace."

Again her staff glowed, and again her eyes glowed bright with fire. Her skin blanched and then took on a pale blue colour. A network of eggshell like cracks spread out across her face. All of a sudden she looked a spitting image of her father.

It was clear that *Cana Dei* had built a stronghold inside her mind at this point, and I didn't know who I could call upon to help her. I found myself thinking about the powerful cat goddess Bastet, who guarded our souls in the Fifth Dimension. She had helped save Seramina from *Cana Dei* during her battle against the warlocks at the Altar of Lore, telling her that journeys towards greatness often begin during our darkest hour.

Somehow, I hoped that Bastet would once again leap out of a portal and tell us what to do next. But it wasn't going to happen – destiny had shown us how things would pan out.

I prowled away from Seramina and went to sit next to Ta'ra by the fire, nestling myself into her warmth. A wind started to pick up outside, buffeting against the walls and howling out in all its fury.

There in the hovel at the end of the worlds, we awaited destiny. Neither Ta'ra nor I purred.

32

DESTINY RISING

It must have been a good hour before destiny announced its arrival, and it didn't even knock on the door. Instead it charged in, in the form of the wind, slamming the door open. The stench of rotten vegetable juice pushed away the sweeter smell of wood smoke. The wind was so strong that it extinguished the fire, and on the distant horizon through the thick purple haze I saw flashes of dry lightning.

Seramina stood up from her perch. There was no fire burning behind her eyes, but still her face had retained that pale blue tinge with eggshell cracks across it. She looked the very image of a powerful warlock, her silver hair flowing over her shoulders as she moved. It didn't look as though she was choosing to walk, but rather as if her staff was pulling her along as it blazed with an energy of its own. As if on its own accord, the crystal seemed to be casting spells into the air, although I had no idea what they were. Every time the crystal pulsed, lightning once again flashed on the horizon. This was clearly the beginning of the end.

Seramina stopped at the door then looked over her shoulder; she spoke with a deep voice that wasn't her own. It rumbled and was charged with dark magic.

"Come," she said in the voice of *Cana Dei*. "Or stay, and let destiny take its course."

She left and my feet felt like lead weights, keeping the rest of my body in place. Ta'ra nudged me forwards with her nose.

"We need to do this," she said. "Come on, Ben. We'll face destiny together."

I swallowed my fear and edged forwards. There was a rocking chair outside on the hovel's porch, just as there had been in the vision. Seramina sat in it, watching the horizon, her staff in her hand. Then came a terrifying feeling of déjà vu, since the words tumbled out of my mouth even though I'd heard myself speak them in many visions before.

"Seramina," I said. "What are you doing?"

"Do not try to stop me, Ben," Seramina replied. "The warlocks are coming, and I will defeat them. This is my chance to finish them."

"No ... you have to stop this. This isn't the way."

"They are coming, Ben. If I stop them, I will save the dimensions."

We both knew that it wasn't true. This was *Cana Dei* speaking through her clenched teeth, and it almost felt as if an external force was controlling the words coming out of my mouth too.

"But why like this?" I asked. "Surely there must be another way."

"There isn't. I will destroy you if you stand in my way, Dragoncat. Now step aside."

The wind as it ruffled my fur felt even colder than it had when I was on Salanraja's back above the Crystal Mountains. A thick layer of cloud had developed in the sky, and across the barren landscape it seemed to be circling, gathering density. All around us the dead husks of trees that decades ago might have lived in this place fought to keep grounded against the wind.

It was so strong I thought it might also carry me away. If it could have blown harder, perhaps it could even have carried Seramina to brighter climes. She was only thin and light after all. But as if rooted by the charged energy of her staff, she remained firmly ensconced in her chair.

The script was over for the time being, and so I had a chance to put in some words of my own.

"There's no one here," I said to Seramina at my place by her knees. "If we walk away now, they might never arrive."

She didn't say anything; she didn't even turn her head to acknowledge me. Her eyes now burned with that wicked fire. Her hair flailed out in all directions, yet it never seemed to lash at her face. A bright aura surrounded her and her skin seeming to glow. Meanwhile the storm continued to rage.

It occurred to me that *Cana Dei* was playing a horrible game with us – it was the only one here who knew about my dilemma. Seramina still clutched her staff in her right hand, her knuckles white. *Cana Dei* was completely in control of her now, and all it need do was to command her to point her staff at me and she could send out a blazing beam that would fry me in seconds. As to why it didn't want to do that, I had no idea, and I still have no idea to this day.

Soon enough the portals arrived out of nowhere, looking like breaks in the distant clouds. With the way that the light shimmered around them, the wind playing with the magic, it was difficult to discern their outlines. I figured there were around twenty.

The golems stepped out first. The premonitions we'd seen had clearly skimped on the details, but there were hundreds of them. Stone golems with massive craggy limbs that could crush anything that got near them; fire golems that could launch themselves in the air as if from catapults and then explode upon impact; forest golems that are born as whirlwinds that suck up natural material until they become great hulking lumps of wood with menacing green eyes; clay golems with a red and a blue crystal eye, capable of melting from one form to the next and with the ability to drown their victims within their substance.

Then came the manipulators, wisps of light with spectral staffs that seemed to float in front of them. As soon as they left the portal, they sent up beams of white light into the air that seemed to cast a slew of bone dragons out of the clouds. Shrieks filled the air, answered again by the terrible cries of the howling wind.

Next came the wargs, stumbling out almost as if tripping over themselves, grunting and growling. They looked upon us with their red menacing eyes, and although they were far away from us, I could sense the hope that one of us would be their next meal.

Last came the warlocks, the five who claimed to serve Lasinta. They arrived in their carrion eater forms – a seagull, a vulture, a buzzard, a bald eagle, and a hawk. Finally came the grunts and wheezes of a condor, though I'm not sure I would have heard them amidst all the noise if it weren't for my spectacular feline hearing.

"It's time," Seramina said, kicking the rocking chair away as she stood up straight.

She stepped forward, and I braced myself for the hardest decision I'd ever have to make in my life, and this time it didn't involve food.

❧ 33 ❧

DESTINY FALLING

Above the rows and rows of magical creatures ready for battle, six birds of prey approached us from the sky. The warlocks had known there was no point in using these forms to attack Seramina. The young teenager was so powerful that she'd reflect their magic right back at them.

If they were going to fight Seramina, they would need to do so six to one.

The bird forms of the five subordinate warlocks plummeted downwards and then crashed into the ground. A plume of purple smoke arose around each of them, and soon they were all in their human forms.

Finally came the giant condor, who landed in front of them all. She sent up a massive explosion of dust and smoke, and then out of it all stepped Lasinta. Even from here I could see the fury in her eyes.

She looked as if she had given up on trying to fight destiny. As though, like almost everyone here, she'd decided it would be easier just to play her part. Our roles had been set, and now it was only a matter of time.

Lasinta stepped forwards, and I realised we were back to our scripted roles.

Seramina's eyes burned with fire as she screamed out at the warlocks: "What do you want, Lasinta? All of you … Why do you have to fight me? All I ever wanted was to be left alone …"

Some of the words were different, I noticed, than what I'd seen before. Already destiny seemed to be shifting in new and unpredictable ways. But still the events all seemed to be converging towards the same outcome.

"You hold too much power," Lasinta said. "You are a threat to our kind, and you are a threat to me. You could have joined us, but it is too late for that now. Young warlock, if I don't destroy you, then you will destroy me."

"If you hadn't come against me," Seramina shouted back, "then none of this may have happened." For a moment, the words seemed to have come from the young teenager herself.

Now we really seemed to be deviating from the script. I also felt power surging through my muscles, and *Cana Dei* was in my mind somewhere, calling to me. I positioned myself around Seramina, ready to make the fated choice.

"Destiny has determined it this way," Lasinta shouted back.

"Yet still you didn't have to come here," Seramina said.

"Oh, but I did! I have hope that there is another path, and that we can win this. We seem to have no other choice, do we?"

"And now I owe you nothing," Seramina said, her voice taking that deep and sonorous timbre once again. *Cana Dei* was back. "You could have had so much power, Lasinta, but you failed me. You have failed us all, and so you shall not claim the prize. I, Seramina, daughter of the failed Astravar, am the vessel who shall rule the worlds."

Together, Seramina and Lasinta both screamed. Seramina swung her staff in a downward arc and the crystal flared with light brighter than a supernova. Lasinta had already seen this move coming – it had been a part of the vision after all – and so she brought her staff down in a graceful move, summoning two purple wisp-dragons out of the sky.

All the other warlocks cast a network of spells of their own, and the sky blazed with dark magic. They gathered their magic into a ball, building energy, and the wisp dragon circled around it gaining in power. All this time Seramina drew more energy into her staff. Distantly, the army of magical creatures shimmered and warped into strange shapes.

She wasn't just creating magic on her own; she was drawing on the army that Lasinta had gathered. The warlocks had been summoning these creatures over a long time, expending years of effort for this single occasion.

Cana Dei, meanwhile, had been planning this all along. Seramina needed an immense amount of power for the destined spell, and the warlocks had brought what she needed right to her front door.

Lasinta let out a loud cry, and the other five warlocks responded with a shout of their own. Together they thrust their staffs forward, and the gigantic magical ball of energy was launched upwards towards Seramina. Because their spell contained such a vast amount of energy, it would take a while to fall upon her. Seramina had around a minute to respond before the mist dragons would eat her alive, leaving nothing but ethereal dust.

Seramina's eyes were now two blazing suns, and her whole body and her hair were aglow. Her hair flailed around her shoulders and those eggshell-cracks had spread even further across her skin. I could see the ravages of years of terror. She had grown afraid of the future, and so I knew I had to act now.

I had no choice. This was destiny.

I summoned my staff bearer. It moved faster than a swift as it plunged the staff into my mouth. The raging horror of betrayal and adrenaline burned through my muscles. But I saw an opening, and Seramina with *Cana Dei* burning inside her turned her head to me, and her lips curled into a wicked grin.

Do it, Dragoncat. The words came unbidden in my head in that commanding rumbling tone. *This is your destiny. Let me take control of your mind.*

My muscles now were surging with power. Time had slowed around me. I got ready to release the spell that would end Seramina. I felt powerful, I felt complete ... I felt as if I could break the worlds.

And then the light was snuffed out of Seramina's eyes. *Cana Dei* had released its grip on her so it could control my mind. Her face fell, and for a brief moment in broken time I saw the innocent teenager I'd known for so long, the young girl who hadn't asked for any of this.

I saw in that young face a friend.

My jaw went slack. My staff dropped from my mouth. It hit the ground and tumbled over the rocks.

"I can't do it," I said.

I waited for the light to return to Seramina's eyes, and for her to finish plunging her staff into the ground, because I knew that my decision would break the world.

"Of course you can't," Ta'ra said from somewhere nearby. In all honesty, I'd forgotten about her. "But you've bought Fairycat enough time to trick destiny."

For the first time, *Cana Dei* had been caught off guard. It took control of Seramina again, and her body spasmed. Then it turned her head, and it said out of her lips in a mocking tone, "With what?"

"With this," Ta'ra said.

She had positioned herself in front of the girl, the bright white diamond marking on her chest catching the glow from Seramina's skin.

Then it all happened at once. A flash of yellow broke the glamour and revealed Ta'ra's staff that was already clutched in her mouth, still only looking like specks of gold dancing around an invisible substance. Then out of it came a paltry yellow spark that hit the crystal on Seramina's staff dead centre.

"Is that all you've got?" Seramina said. "So little power against the most powerful force in all the dimensions?"

The girl had already completed the motion to thrust her staff downwards, and the base of it smashed into the ground. The ground rumbled, and I waited for it to split apart. I waited for it all to end.

Instead there came another yellow flash from Seramina's staff, which dissolved into what looked like hundreds of thousands of motes of fairy dust. These hovered in place for a moment until out of them hatched butterflies, so many of them in myriad colours.

"Oh," Ta'ra said, "I forgot to mention the butterflies."

It wasn't yet over. From above the static pulled on my fur, and I looked up to see that the magical ball of energy was almost upon us. Now Ta'ra and I had also moved within its radius, and I knew I couldn't act fast enough to destroy it.

Ta'ra lifted her head and from her staff came a much brighter yellow beam that hit the magical globe straight on. The subsequent spell worked much faster than the last; the great magical globe's purple outline shimmered, and then it turned to yellow dust. The same happened to the mist dragons, and out of the whole display emerged a much larger swarm of butterflies than the first.

"And more butterflies," Ta'ra said.

By this point, the light had completely gone from

Seramina's eyes. Her face was now blanched of colour, and it had at least lost that cracked appearance. She looked down at where the staff had been in her hands. The butterflies that had replaced it flocked around her for a moment, then they lifted and joined the larger swarm. Together they headed north to where there were flowers and pollen aplenty.

That was when a little colour rushed into Seramina's cheeks, and she parted her lips in slight O. Her mouth widened more, and out came a loud a hearty laugh. It was a long laugh, full of relief and tears. But she wasn't the only one laughing. From beyond us, at the head of the massive magical army, Lasinta cackled away.

34

COUP

I'd never heard a warlock laughing so hard, and I'm not talking now about Seramina – I no longer considered her a warlock. I'm talking about the elderly Lasinta, who approached with her hands held to her waist cackling as she did so. The other warlocks approached with caution, and behind them their whole army stood on standby. Despite Ta'ra's recent spell bringing a slight scent of honey and the Faerie Realm, the horrid odour of rotten vegetable juice had returned. The Darklands were still an evil place; that much hadn't changed.

Fortunately, Seramina's powerful spell had sucked the magic out of the entire army of magical creations that the warlocks had brought with them. Only their crystal hearts and the bodies of the wargs lying on the ground behind them remained. Still, the teenager seemed to have spent all her energy, and I doubted Ta'ra and I would be able to take down six warlocks alone.

"*Hang on, Bengie,*" Salanraja said in my head, her voice coming from a distant plane. "*We'll be there soon.*"

"*Salanraja,*" I replied, not even concerned about the fact she'd just called me Bengie. "*You're back...*"

"*The crystals stopped time around us for a while,*" Salanraja said. "*They needed you to get Seramina over to the Darklands so you could do what you needed to do. Then they showed us what happened in their facets. We watched Seramina about to battle the warlocks, and when Ta'ra turned her staff into butterflies ... We dragons laughed so loud that for a moment it looked like the caverns might fall. It was all a trick, Bengie. You tricked Cana Dei.*"

"*Well, Ta'ra did,*" I said.

"*I guess in a way the crystals did. They were on our side all along. You know, even I had my doubts about them.*"

I suppose we'd all had our doubts really. I still wonder to this day whether the breaking of the Great Crystal in the first place had been part of the plan – and also if the whole thing hadn't worked, how far the crystals would be planning to go to manipulate *Cana Dei.*

"*How will you get here?*" I asked Salanraja.

"*The crystals will soon summon a portal. There's a giant crystal in an adjacent chamber that has shown us what we need to do.*"

"*So how long?*" I asked. The warlocks had almost reached us now, Lasinta still cackling away and the other warlocks watching her with wary eyes as if they thought she'd gone mad.

"*Soon ... They just need to restore the fabric of space-*"

time here to its normal state, and then we'll be on our way."

She was cut off, and I watched the mad elderly warlock traipse closer. All we needed to do, it seemed, was buy some time and convince the warlocks not to destroy us. With most humans I would have thought this easy – we cats are particularly good at persuasion tactics, with our cute wide eyes and soft voices at our disposal, which can get even the harshest of subjects to bend to our will. But these were evil warlocks we were talking about. Cute strategies generally don't tend to work on evil people.

When Lasinta was within speaking range she addressed us with a loud voice, only just managing to contain her laughter. "Oh dear, oh dear. In my whole career I'd never have thought I'd laugh so hard. Yet here we are."

Seramina by this point had collapsed into a slump on the rocking chair, all her energy completely drained away. There was no sign of *Cana Dei* left in her. She now looked a helpless and exhausted girl.

Still, she looked up at Lasinta with distrusting eyes. Ta'ra and I also watched her cautiously, our staffs clenched in our mouths. I wasn't sure what chance we'd have against the six most powerful known warlocks, but at least we could put up a fight.

"All this time," Lasinta continued, "I thought we had no way out. And yet you found a way to best destiny. We won with flying colours it seems." She cackled with laughter once again. "Now you won't destroy the world, and I have no need to destroy you, Seramina, daughter of Astravar, though I can see why you might hate your heritage."

I wanted to say something, but I had my staff in my mouth. Ta'ra did too. Fortunately, Seramina had enough spirit within her to speak for all of us. "What are you proposing?" she asked.

This time, Lasinta only let out a slight chuckle. "You know, I've known about your little prophecy even before you were born. I was only your age when I started on the path that would lead to me becoming a warlock, and I thought I had no other choice. *Cana Dei* showed me the prophecy we're all familiar with. My warlock comrades here each have a similar story, each of us thinking that if we didn't do something to stop it that it would end us. Thus we let the dark force control us, and what you have just done ... You have proven that there is another way."

I half expected to see the fire return to Seramina's narrowed eyes, but they remained vacant. She shook her head and said nothing. I had nothing to say to her either, not after everything she'd done. Ta'ra spoke in our place. She needed to let the staff bearer lift the staff out of her mouth to do so. I still held mine, though, but I wasn't sure how exactly I might defend us all with it should the warlocks choose to attack.

"So what are you proposing?" she asked.

"Perhaps we can negotiate another peace treaty with your king?" Lasinta said.

"As I remember," Ta'ra said, "you failed to uphold the last peace treaty. Why should we trust you now?"

As if to indicate she was no longer a threat, Lasinta bent over and placed her staff on the ground. The faint glow in its crystal faded, as if the earth wanted to pull its magic away. Lasinta showed Seramina her palms. "I hope the king shall grant amnesty to all of us. I don't want to fight anymore – I'm old and I've grown tired of it. I hope the King's Dragon Guard and the White Guard will allow us all to live our remaining lives in peace."

Her last word hung in the air, a break in the wind allowing it to linger. For a moment I thought that was the end of it all. Salanraja and I could retire in our country cottage with Seramina and Ange, and perhaps Rine could visit sometimes if he didn't bring Bellari.

But something was wrong – I could smell the rotten stench of it, and the hackles rose on the back of my neck. Meanwhile, purple gas began to seep out of the cracks in the ground in front of us.

It took me a moment to see the exact nature of the problem, because the glow in the other five warlocks' eyes was faint. Still the fire burned at the back of them. The flame of *Cana Dei*.

Moonz, the elderly man who was almost as old as Lasinta, stepped forward to speak. He used no voice that I'd heard him use before. Instead, the timbre was much deeper and rumbled with evil intent.

"So that's what you want, Lasinta," he said. "You have proven yourself a traitor, never worthy to join our cause."

Lasinta turned her face towards him, and her eyes went wide with terror.

Ritrad, the giant muscular male warlock spoke next. The fire at the back of his eyes, and all the warlocks' eyes for that matter, had grown much more intense. His voice sounded just as laced with evil as Moonz. "You thought you could best destiny."

"You thought you could walk the path of *Cana Dei* without becoming one of us," said Cala, the red haired and vibrant looking female warlock.

"You thought you could have it all," said Junas – he was the tall and lanky one.

"Now this is our final gift to you," said Pladana. She was small and wiry.

In unison, the five warlocks whipped forward their staffs. Out of them shot five purple smelly beams, all of them centred on the breast pocket of Lasinta's robe. Beneath this, her fragile heart beat its very few last beats.

I can never forget the terror I saw on her face before she dissolved into dust. But I didn't have long to even think about feeling sorry for her, because the five remaining warlocks had now turned to face us.

"We are servants of *Cana Dei*," they said together, their lips moving in sync as if they were part of a choir, "and for eternity we remain loyal to the darkness." Their gazes turned upon Seramina. "Young warlock, you had a chance to join us. Now it is time for you to die."

Whiskers, we'd come so far, and I had thought we were all going to walk away from these lands unscathed. But fierce expressions on each of the warlocks' faces made me realise *Cana Dei* was angry.

I summoned magic into my staff, my muscles

burning with energy. I had no idea whom to target. In all honesty, I thought that moment would be my last.

But that very same moment, the crystals of the Versta Caverns took the opportunity to open the portals that would let my brave feline allies, the newly initiated dragon riders, flood in.

35

ALLIES

There must have been a good two-dozen portals that opened behind us, and the first to emerge from out of them was Max on Corralsa.

His barks cut the air apart as he screamed, "Wargs! Wargs!" He hesitated. "What happened to all the wargs?"

Then he summoned his staff bearer, which materialised out of thin air and plunged Max's staff in his mouth. Olan came next with Aleam. Rine, Bellari, Ange, and Kamino followed on their dragons in close pursuit.

But the most prominent arrival of them all was Matharon, heralded by his mighty roar. It sent the ground shaking around us, and after it had subsided, I heard the discarded crystals tinkle.

The white Abyssinian emerged on her black dwarf dragon, Gratis. Behind her came Kada and Salanraja, who separated from the flock and stopped hovering over us as if to protect us.

Meanwhile, magic flooded into the warlocks' staffs

and the fires of *Cana Dei* blazed even brighter in their eyes. I could see that they thought they could defeat such a small a force. They were after all powerful magicians, and only Aleam matched the might of any one of them.

But clearly *Cana Dei* hadn't expected the convoy of dragon riding cats to emerge out of the remaining portals. Together, their half-sized dragons filled the sky, and to my surprise each cat had a staff in its mouth, burning brightly at the tip.

This I thought mightily unfair, and again I found myself wondering what the crystals were up to. It had taken me months to get my staff and to be able to cast powerful magic. Now the crystals just seemed to be handing out staffs willy-nilly like cat treats.

Together the dragons roared, and the warlocks each released a spell into the air. Five mist dragons formed, launching upwards. These cut across the path of the swarm of charging dragons, causing them to wheel around.

Their magic was just a diversion, for soon a plume of smoke emerged from each warlock in turn.

"You may think you've defeated us," Cala said, and I saw the last vision of her red swirling hair before she transformed into her carrion-eater form, a hawk.

"Because it seems that destiny has favoured your actions today," the muscular giant, Ritrad said, before he transformed into a vulture.

"Yet this is not the end, for there still must be a battle to come." These words came from the tall lanky man, Junas, who then became a buzzard.

"For I, *Cana Dei*, have now claimed the souls of these five warlocks. Together we have the power to break the worlds." The small wiry warlock, Pladana, uttered this threat, and she presently turned into a broad-winged hawk.

Moonz was the last of them all to transform, and did so into a bald eagle. Together the five carrion-eaters took off into the dark cover of the clouds. It wasn't long before they disappeared behind the murk.

The dragons and their riders above had just finished dealing with the mist-dragons. Magic flashed across the sky for a moment – lightning tearing through the clouds, this time not a part of the storm but summoned by Aleam.

For a moment all was calm, and then the dragons together let out piercing roars. My ears flattened against my head, and I looked up at Salanraja. Her yellow eyes gleamed. The dwarf dragons carrying their cat riders swooped downwards, and to my surprise the cats dropped their staffs out of their mouths. They had each aimed their staffs in such a way that they tumbled onto a pile, one after another.

After enough staffs had fallen, the pile exploded into flame. As the cats dropped more staffs onto the pile, the fire built, its flames licking at the gravid clouds. I gazed at this in stunned astonishment.

"*Salanraja, what the whiskers are they doing?*" I said in my mind. "*They're destroying their staffs.*"

Salanraja laughed. "*They're not staffs – they're sticks with fire on the end. You might call them torches.*"

"Torches? You mean to say they've not got their staffs yet?"

"It's much too early to give these dragon rider Initiates their staffs, Bengie ... This was Matharon's plan. Once the crystals showed us in a vision that you were to battle five warlocks, we knew we didn't have enough mages to defeat them. We thought if we get enough straight branches from some of the dwarf pine trees at the bottom of the mountains and set their ends on fire then they'd look just like staffs from the ground. I bet it made our small force look much greater than it actually was."

"But you have so many dragons. Wouldn't they have been enough to defeat the warlocks?"

"And warlocks know spells that can shield them from any aerial attack, which would have given them time to destroy you three and then fly off. That's why dragons need dragon riders; to help balance the odds."

I blinked in disbelief, appreciating the warmth emanating from the fire. *Cana Dei*, it seemed, had been tricked once again.

Ta'ra came up next to me and pushed her nose up to mine. "We should get out of here," she said. "Let's fly back to Dragonsbond Academy."

"We should," I said, and then before she had a chance to turn around, I added, "thank you, Ta'ra."

"Whatever for?"

"For saving me. If you hadn't been here, supporting me all this time, I'm not sure I would have done the right thing."

"I think you would have, Ben," she said. "In fact, I know you would."

At that moment Kada landed, and my former Cat Sidhe companion turned in a circle and scurried up onto his back. Hallinar came down next, and Seramina gained a surprising boost of energy long enough for her to clamber up to the saddle on her dragon's back. Salanraja touched down soon after that, and without thinking I rushed up her tail and found my place within her corridor of spikes. She lifted me up into the sky, and the dragons carried their feline riders out of the Darklands and back towards our much more verdant home.

36

THE RETURN

We left the Darklands and flew over the Wastelands, a convoy of several dragon riding humans, a dragon riding dog, and a couple of hundred dragon riding cats. We were high enough that I didn't catch even a whiff of rotten vegetable juice. Instead, the wind brought a fresh breeze from the north, almost as if it wanted to push away the atmosphere of the tainted lands and replace them with freshness and life.

The Wastelands were a no-man's land, where neither citizens of the Darklands nor those of Illumine Kingdom tended to roam. Most of the plants that I could see from up here, hugging the fringes of the foetid swamps, were tainted in some way by dark magic. Without it they wouldn't be able to survive in such acidic soil.

I'd first encountered them when I'd fled from Astravar's tower, after he'd imprisoned me there so many months ago. I'd remembered little of my passing through it, but now flying above it evoked flashbacks of how scared I'd been of this alien world full of magic and dark-ness that I'd now come to know so well.

I now felt most comfortable on my perch on Salanra-ja's back, glad that I didn't have to travel any of the way back on foot. Seramina was flying slightly ahead of us on Hallinar, next to Aleam's Olan and Max's Corralsa, with Matharon in tow. Salanraja had told me that the three great dragons wanted to watch over her, just in case, though I don't know what she could do any more. Ta'ra had turned her staff into butterflies, which she would have to chase to the ends of the earth to get back. There was no chance of her causing any more chaos now.

In my mind it was also as if a veil had lifted. I no longer seemed to hear the voice of *Cana Dei* muttering in there. In a way, I felt like the naughty cat who had disap-pointed its master and wasn't getting any dinner that evening, but that was silly. Cats who don't want to live with their masters or mistresses tend to run away. The old Ragamuffin back home had told me he'd met quite a few cats of the Alhambra who had been in such circum-stances. Humans called them strays, but we called them adventurers – cats who had decided to forgo living in relative comfort to explore the wilds and learn to live like their ancestors. Apparently in the Fourth Dimension they had inspired quite a few human authors, who had written whole canons of children's books about them.

The rest of the dragons from Dragonsbond Academy followed the larger dragons in a tight row. Salanraja and I were part of this sub-formation, as were the four teenaged Initiates and Esme's and Ta'ra's dwarf dragons,

Gratis and Kada. The remaining dwarf dragons and their cat dragon riders rode at the back of the formation in rows of three or four, forming a long tail.

I was so enjoying the journey that I didn't notice the time passing. Soon enough we had reached the fringes between the Wastelands and Illumine Kingdom, signified by a massive and semi-transparent magical barrier that extended from east to west. It glowed bright blue, from the ground up to the point it hit the clouds, where it sparkled and dissipated. Since the warlocks had broken their peace treaty, the White Guard had re-erected this to keep any dark magical creations out. Though I guess it had been rendered useless by the fact that the warlocks had now become powerful enough that they could summon a portal to take them anywhere.

Still, White Mages stood on the other side of it atop their unicorns, placed at intervals all along the length of the barrier. They held their staffs up high above their heads, and both the crystals along the length of the wooden canes and the unicorns' horns glowed brightly, feeding energy into the barrier. I could only just see them through the shimmering surface, watching us from below as we approached. The barrier hummed like a thousand wasps, and for a moment I thought they might not let us through.

But the dragons carried straight on along their course. Meanwhile one of the White Guards gestured at us with his staff, and then several White Mages lowered their weapons. Both their staffs and their unicorns' horns stopped glowing, and we passed through the barrier without incident.

That was when Matharon turned away from us, and he roared out a command to the dwarf dragons following behind. The great bronze dragon of legend, and the dragons and their feline riders under his tutelage, broke off from the formation. They turned towards the mountains in the northeast.

"*Where the whiskers are they going?*" I asked. "*I thought we were all a team now.*"

Salanraja let out a deep laugh that sent her body rumbling under my feet. "*I'm sorry, I often forget to tell you things, Bengie. They're off back to Bestian Academy to complete their training. No more cats in the Dragonsbond Academy cattery, I'm afraid.*"

"*Then what about us? Why don't we follow them?*"

"*And here I was thinking you hated the mountains and the snow.*"

"*I do, but still, I thought I could help them a little. Who better to teach them how to become powerful dragon riding cats than the great Dragoncat, descendant of the great Asian leopard cat and the mighty George, vanquisher of warlocks and eluder of Cana Dei itself?*"

"*You do go on, don't you, Bengie?*"

"*What do you expect, when I'm so heroic? I really think we should go with them. All of us.*"

"*But we have to return to Dragonsbond Academy. There's something waiting for us there – can't you feel it?*"

"*Feel what?*"

"*Well, I guess it's going to be a surprise for you.*

Although you might want to say goodbye to Seramina first."

She craned her head downwards, to where a convoy of White Mages were waiting on the road with their unicorns. A wagon stood on the road between them, pulled by regular horses, one black and the other a brown dun.

I recognised the White Mage standing at the front of them, characterised by her short red hair and stern gaze that I could feel from here, even though she was so far away.

"Alliander!" I said. *"We can't give Seramina back to her."*

"Why not?" Salanraja said. *"The situation is different now. Seramina has had a long talk with Hallinar on her journey back. He and all the other dragons think it's the best thing. Seramina does, too."*

"But Alliander will throw her in prison or make her do a thousand squats every day, or one of her other horrible punishments."

"No, she won't ... Alliander has already liaised with Seramina through a network of nearby dragons. She's agreed to put her in fine accommodation, so long as she never uses magic again or tries to obtain another staff. Seramina will live the life of a normal teenage girl in Cimlean City, much as she wanted to when she first started out."

I growled; I really didn't feel Seramina deserved any of this. She was perhaps the most powerful magician who'd ever lived. But then if she wanted it, who was I to try and stop her? I thought about my dreams of retirement, of how Seramina and I were meant to train together and eventually go and live in a cottage in the countryside. But now she would live somewhere else, and I thought I might never see her again. I was being separated from her just like I'd been separated from my master and mistress back in my original home of South Wales.

"You know how it is, Bengie," Salanraja said. *"We need to go back to Dragonsbond Academy and report to the Council of Three about what has happened. I'm not going to let you get out of your duties so easily, not while there are still five warlocks at large."*

I growled again, but I had nothing else to say to Salanraja. Besides, we were just about coming in to land.

37

FAMILY

Hallinar flew with Seramina ahead of the formation, and only Salanraja with me, Kada with Ta'ra, and the great white dragon Olan with Aleam, followed. I guess no one else had built a strong bond with the teenage girl. Seramina had always been a bit of a recluse by nature. She was a lot younger than any of the other humans at Dragonsbond Academy, which I guess had made it a little difficult for her to fit in.

Salanraja's flying was slow and graceful, and the air grew warmer as we approached the ground. She landed, and the scent of pine trees and grass hit my nostrils. I can't express how much I appreciated that; back in the Darklands I had truly believed I would never smell normal life again.

Seramina was standing beside the grey Hallinar, watching me with a vacant stare. She didn't hold my gaze long when I looked back at her though, averting her eyes to instead gaze at the long grass. Her arms hung low as if she didn't want to hold on to her body anymore; clearly she was ashamed of who she was at this moment. The girl who had tried to break the worlds, but she wasn't the one who should be held responsible for it. Everything that had happened had been due to the machinations of *Cana Dei*, a force far stronger than she'd been at her strongest. After all she'd only been its conduit, channelling its power.

I stalked over to provide her some comfort. I didn't get far before Ta'ra strode up next to me, smelling of fairy dust and looking like a mighty proud cat if I'd ever seen one. I stopped to look at my faithful *companion* a moment, and she touched her nose to mine.

"Are you okay, Ben?" she asked.

I exhaled a deep breath, somehow not having realised how much I'd been holding in. I looked once again at Seramina, who was now watching Alliander trotting towards her on Tanni, her unicorn.

"I'm okay," I replied, "but I'm not so sure about Seramina. Have you heard what they're doing, Ta'ra? They're arresting her!"

Ta'ra let out a soft and comforting meow. "I don't think it's quite like that. Seramina's doing this willingly, and it's probably for the best for everyone."

"How can you say that? After all you've been through together."

Ta'ra shot me a stern glance. "So what? Do you think we should send her back to Dragonsbond Academy? Just to feel how out of place she would be with all those other students using magic? Then there'd be the temptation to call on *Cana Dei* again."

"But maybe she *could* learn how to use it. Finally learn how to control it."

"We've tried that already, and you've seen how it ends. You know this is for the best ... I know you do."

She was right, in a way, although I didn't like it. In my old life as a regular cat I'd never known the concept of sacrifice. There were no hard decisions – I'd either hunted or hadn't hunted, slept or hadn't slept, groomed or hadn't groomed.

"Come on," Ta'ra said. "We came down here to say goodbye, didn't we?"

"Yeah," I said, and I followed her through the long grass.

Seramina turned her head to regard Ta'ra and me as we approached. For a moment she looked as if she was going to bend down and stroke us. But her posture suggested she didn't even think herself worthy of that action.

"I'm so sorry," she said, her eyes wet with tears. "I thought I could make something of my life."

I rubbed my body against her leg and then lay down next to her foot. Ta'ra lay down next to me. Both of us remained silent, because we sensed she had more to say. Her words came out in sputtered gasps.

"I thought I could be someone else, other than the daughter of the most powerful and evillest warlock. Someone good ... Not an even more powerful and even more evil *warlock*." She took a deep breath. "I'll be better in Cimlean city. I'll be decent. Lead a normal life ..."

I chirped gently, hoping that it would comfort her. "You did the best you could. No one was forced to handle what you had to handle. If you return to Dragonsbond Academy, I think everyone would understand."

"But you know why I can't, don't you?" Seramina said. "Of course you do. They've promised me a better life. I can do better ..."

Alliander had her unicorn rear and halted only metres away. Tanni let out a soft bray and munched the grass as if she wanted to leave Seramina to her business. I glared at him, not trusting his intentions for a minute. There was something off about that beast, just like there was something off about his mistress.

Aleam had also reached us by this point. His eyes looked tired and he moved slower than I remembered. Clearly all this adventuring had taken its toll on him.

"Seramina," he said. "All this time I've guarded you, and all this time I knew what the crystals knew. You mustn't blame yourself. You did well to keep *Cana Dei* out for as long as you did."

"But I could have done better," Seramina argued.

"Perhaps," Aleam said. "And there are days that you shall do better, and days that you shall do worse. But just know that I'm proud of how far you've come. Though your decision is hard, I know why you need to make it. It's a sign of growing up, though I do regret you might have done so too fast."

Seramina blinked some more tears from her eyes. She

wiped them away with the back of her hand, then she leaned forward and folded herself into Aleam's embrace.

"Will you come and visit?" she asked. "All of you? Ben and Ta'ra, I want to know what powerful magicians you will become. And I'll miss you ... Thank you for carrying me this far."

Aleam chuckled. "That's what friends are for," he said.

"More than just friends," Seramina said. "We're family ..."

I purred and meowed as I nestled closer to Seramina. Family ... I liked the sound of that. We would all be family forever.

38

A PLEASANT SURPRISE

Salanraja had mentioned there'd be a surprise waiting for me in Dragonsbond Academy, and indeed there was. Needless to say I was a little disappointed at first – I mean, I'd thought by the way that Salanraja had presented it, and continued to tease me about the surprise on the journey home, that the Council of Three or someone else in power might have managed to procure some smoked salmon from the Fourth Dimension.

After all, Salanraja had stated, *"It's something that you've been missing and you never thought would return."*

It had been quite some time since I'd had a meal of the stuff. It was the last thing I'd eaten before Astravar had rudely passed his hands through a portal and yanked me into this world, away from my breakfast. Honestly, I couldn't think what else it could be, and by the time Salanraja and the other dragons touched down in the inner bailey, I was salivating.

Alas, it wasn't smoked salmon waiting for me there,

just some strands of roast duck that Matron Canda had kindly plucked from the kitchen's leftovers and put down in four bowls on the ground. She'd clearly realised that Max, Esme, Ta'ra and I would be ravenous when we arrived.

She was right. My nose guided me straight to the food, and I must have eaten the whole thing in less than a minute. The sun blazed down overhead, strong for late autumn. Sparrows chirped in a nearby elm tree, and the air had a magical type of freshness to it as if nothing in Dragonsbond Academy had changed. Students milled about on their business, dashing to classes, and I could hear the calls of Driar Gallant, the quartermaster, instructing students in how to use their staffs as physical weapons, should they ever need it.

Despite the pleasantness of it all, I felt rather cheated. I mean I'd had plenty of roast duck in the First Dimension, but only once here had I eaten smoked salmon.

"*What's the matter?*" Salanraja asked in my mind. "*I thought you'd be happy to finally get something to eat.*"

"*I am. But the way that you described it, I thought it was going to be something special.*"

Salanraja laughed. "*Like smoked salmon, you mean? Well, at least your appetite has returned.*"

"*It has. I can now eat normal food again, and I will do so for the rest of my life.*"

"*Bengie, Bengie, Bengie. It's not the food I was talking about as the surprise. I'm really amazed you can't feel it.*"

My ears perked up and I took a sniff of the air, trying to work out what she was talking about. I heard Rine and

Bellari nearby giggling about something. Really, I didn't know what she'd done to the boy, and I was beginning to wonder if she was a warlock herself with a special ability to cause some kind of love magic. All this time, Rine had been under her spell. On the other side of the bailey, Ange stood with her leg crooked against a wall, reading a book. She didn't seem to be paying the newly engaged couple any heed at all.

"*Nope,*" I said. "*It all still smells of roast duck. No salmon, smoked or otherwise, anywhere.*"

"*You're doing it again. You're making this about your stomach.*"

"*Then what should I be sniffing for?*"

"*Really, you can't feel it?*"

"*Feel what?*"

"*Something different … A change in the fabric of space-time.*"

I tried to focus. For the first time I used my sight, which isn't the first sense cats usually turn to, particularly when confronted by a bowl full of food. The other three animals had left me now, and I wondered for a moment where they might have gone. Then I noticed it: a glow coming from the central courtyard, illuminating the neatly mown blades of grass. From that direction, Max was panting in happy gasps.

"It's beautiful," he said. "It's beautiful. Even better than the last one."

Whiskers, how could I have missed it?

"*The Great Crystal … It's returned.*"

"*Not quite,*" Salanraja said. "*It's a new one that appar-*"

ently materialised in the Central Courtyard right after you tricked Cana Dei *and the warlocks.*"

"*All by itself?*" I asked.

"*Well, no, I'm guessing the crystals worked together to send it here. Or maybe it was here all along.*"

"*So if they could send the crystal to us all along, why didn't they do that in the first place? There would have been no need for anything that happened.*"

Salanraja let out a breathy sigh. "*Probably the future needed to unfold this way for you and Ta'ra to save the day like you did,*" she suggested. "*But who knows in what mysterious ways the crystals work. I'm guessing they had reasons for it.*"

"*They were probably watching us all from their place in the Ninth Dimension, delighting in their little game,*" I said, remembering something *Cana Dei* had mentioned.

"*You what?*"

"*Nothing,*" I said, and I left the food bowl and Salanraja to see our new spectacle.

It wasn't just the Great Crystal that had returned to us. Now that Salanraja had mentioned it, I could also feel the presence of the crystal that belonged to the two of us. I could almost feel it, in fact, pulsing softly with light in Salanraja's chamber. I don't know how to explain it – it was just there like one's breath or heartbeat. You didn't notice it until you focused on it, and then you couldn't help but wonder how you'd missed it.

I kept an image of our crystal in my mind as I entered the central courtyard. It dissipated as I caught a whiff of dog, then the sweeter aroma of cat. On the lawn ahead of me, Max, Esme and Ta'ra were sitting staring upwards in rapt fascination. Their gazes were set on the new Great Crystal that hovered in its regular place above the dais. It was only slightly larger than its predecessor, in other words probably around the size of a small elephant. Beneath this and just at the foot of the dais, the three Great Driars of the Council of Three stood, their hands on their hips and their heads also craned upwards.

It wasn't until I'd sat down next to Ta'ra, my tail swishing gently through the short grass, that I registered exactly what had enthralled them.

"Look, Ben," Ta'ra said to me. "It seems like you're famous. The legend of the mighty Dragoncat revealed at last."

Indeed, the Great Crystal had chosen to display me as the focus of the vision in its wide angular facets. I was travelling at night, lit by a large full moon. I had my staff in my mouth while sailing through the clouds on Salan-raja's back. It glowed white, no yucky trace of *Cana Dei* to be seen in its magic anywhere. In fact, I was casting white magic, and I could tell by the fact that the staff didn't have just one crystal but many, glowing along its length. Out of them streamed what must have been thousands of strands of light fountaining outwards, casting an impressive lightshow that blazed even brighter than those terrifying fireworks humans liked to set off in the Fourth Dimension.

But I wasn't just casting magic. The view in the crystal zoomed out to show the squadron of dragons that I led through the sky. They were all dwarf dragons, and they all carried cats upon their backs as riders. The view twisted downwards to reveal the snow-capped peaks and gaping cave mouths of the Crystal Mountains. On one plateau I could see Bestian Academy, though it was some distance away.

"Commander Dragoncat," Ta'ra said, pride in her voice. "It looks like you're destined to lead an army."

"It does," I said, trepidation rising in my heart.

"*Ah,*" Salanraja said in my mind. "*You've also discovered the news.*"

"*What news?*" I asked.

"*I've just been talking to Matharon. He says that you, Esme, Ta'ra, Max and your dragons need to return to Bestian Academy. The crystals have deemed you worthy to step up to the plate and start training the dragon riding cats.*"

"*Great,*" I said, and I let out a low and guttural growl.

Just as one adventure had ended, it seemed like another was beginning. I had a strong feeling that the remaining warlocks had something to do with it – after all, *Cana Dei* had promised it would get its revenge. By channelling the power of the five remaining warlocks, it had promised, it would still attempt to break the worlds.

I turned away from the vision and instead got to work on grooming Ta'ra's fur. She still tasted a little of rotten vegetable juice, and so she needed a good clean. Perhaps tomorrow Salanraja and I would have to travel, leaving our comrades in Dragonsbond Academy to fend for themselves. Yet for today I was going to enjoy being a normal cat.

Also a descendant of the great Asian leopard cat and the mighty George, I must add. And fate had decided that I would command an army of dragon riding cats.

In other words, it looked like my retirement was going to have to wait.

ACKNOWLEDGMENTS

I wanted to say thank you to the usual team, including Tarryn Thomas for editing and proofreading, my family, particularly my parents for their continuing support and my dear wife Ola for reading early drafts and providing valuable input.

Also, thank you as always to my ARC team. I really appreciate all the work that you put in helping to promote my novels.

Finally, thank you to every single reader – I appreciate everything that you do to support authors and the world of literature at large.

THANK YOU FOR READING *"A Cat's Guide to Vanquishing Evil"*. I hope that you enjoyed it and that it added value for you in your every day life.

I have written a prequel novelette to this series entitled *"A Cat's Guide to Serving a Warlock"*, which you can download for free by signing up to my newsletter at https://chrisbehrsin.com/servingawarlock.

I send bi-monthly emails with promos, giveaways, information about new releases and news about what's going on in my life in general.